I0764629

THE GOSPEL LABYRINTH

Novels by Dennis Bowen

International Thriller Series

THE WATER DIAMONDS
Book 1

THE BLACKSTONE PERFECTION
Book 2

THE CRYSTAL SEDUCTION
Book 3

THE REDROCK QUARANTINE
Book 4

THE FINAL MASQUERADE
Book 5

THE VIRTUE TRANSITION
Book 6

THE JASMINE NEGATIVE
Book 7

THE GOSPEL LABYRINTH
Book 8

The Backstory Files

STONES
Book 1

THE GOSPEL LABYRINTH

Dennis Bowen

The Gospel Labyrinth is a work of fiction. Names, characters, places, and incidents are the products of the author's imagination or are used fictitiously. Any resemblance to actual events, locales, or persons, living or dead, is entirely coincidental.

ISBN: 978-1-7360262-0-5

www.facebook.com/DennisBowenThrillers

www.twitter.com/DBowenThrillers

www.DennisBowen.com

Book Interior Design by 52Novels

ACKNOWLEDGMENTS

Thank you to the readers who have immersed themselves in my *International Thriller Series*. While I create the intrigues that span the globe and enjoy every minute of it, in the end, I write these novels for you and your enjoyment. It's really that simple.

As with *The Water Diamonds*, *The Blackstone Perfection*, *The Crystal Seduction*, *The Redrock Quarantine*, *The Final Masquerade*, *The Virtue Transition*, and *The Jasmine Negative*, my appreciation and gratitude goes out to those who offered suggestions and encouragement during the writing of *The Gospel Labyrinth*.

I express appreciation to my fabulous editor, Laura Taylor. She has provided the editing prowess to insure a quality presentation for this series and for STONES of *The Backstory Files*.

As in life, each successive endeavor—such as writing a series of novels—is built on what came before. Any errors or omissions in *The Gospel Labyrinth* I claim as my own.

Once again, I extend my gratitude to family members and friends for their support, and to former colleagues, some of whom offered up their lives in the service of this great country, and whose presence in my life gives my *International Thriller Series* its noted sense of reality. Thank you to all.

—Dennis Bowen

CHAPTER 1

He followed her. Through a labyrinth of secret tunnels and passageways. It was as if she'd seen plans, and possessed a photographic memory. Or, she'd been here before.

The granite walls were cold, dark, and damp. Small wonder they'd passed rows of laid up wine bottles. He'd stopped to examine a few. Mouton-Rothschild. 1982. At least one hundred of them. It spoke money. No. It screamed wealth.

She turned and pointed to their path ahead.

A set of five stairs leading up. To an oak door replete with elaborate iron hinges.

She made a motion of pulling the door ring, and then fluttered her fingers next to her ear.

An alarm? No. The door would creak like one.

She gestured for him to quickly pull it open, while she stood poised to jump into the room on the other side.

Up went her hand. Three. Two. One. *Now!*

He pulled with all his might.

The door, well-balanced and greased, opened so easily, it slammed him against the wall. He nearly lost his .40 caliber SIG-Sauer pistol. By the time he recovered and stepped through, she stood inside.

Three surprised men, dressed in camouflage, went for their sidearms.

His diminutive companion fired three silenced rounds, hitting each guard in a vital spot. All down. Hard.

Called in at the last minute for the op, he'd just been lightly read in. By a man calling himself Jack. And the man's partner, a blonde he introduced as Marli.

He checked out the room and saw nothing but opulence. As if they'd entered a palace of some sort. Working their way here on a moonless, starless night had given him no clue as to the target venue.

She checked the first two for pulses. None. The third wasn't quite gone yet.

"Not enough blood," she concluded in her native Dutch.

His language skills had culminated with college English. He just watched.

"Breed and bleed," she continued.

She pulled a smaller caliber weapon from her black tactical outfit, placing its barrel to one side of the man's neck. The .22 caliber Beretta puffed once through its own silencer.

The direct hit on the man's carotid artery yielded the expected spurts of thick, red fluid.

"Oh, c'mon," she said in perfect colloquial English.

As if she had not a moment to lose, she placed the pistol on the floor and began CPR.

The blood fairly leaped from the man's neck wound.

She smiled, engaging a pair of cute point dimples on her cheeks.

Her partner's breathing ramped.

Then … it hit him.

The pieces came together.

They were breaking into a royal palace.

Monaco.

His first op since graduating.

From the Farm.

The Company's training ground.

CIA neophyte Magus Crayle muttered to himself, "They paired me with a psychopath."

He was right.

• • •

Crayle sat up. Bolt upright.

His pounding heart seemed seconds away from fibrillation. There was darkness all right, but no bodies. No blood. No diminutive psychopathic CIA operative.

That one was really bad, even for a nightmare.

CHAPTER 2

It was a different day. The very first sound Crayle heard upon waking was a quite familiar whoosh, unique to the three tail mounted jet engines of a Dassault Falcon. He'd even learned to differentiate the 7X from the 8X. Not a problem lately after Lenny Lipschitz commandeered the 7 in Paris, taking out a nuclear-tipped missile bound for Mecca. By his heroic actions, he'd thwarted the insane scheme of former Iranian president and Illuminé madman, Grand Ayatollah Doreihmi Fahsolah. That plane had been destroyed in the blast.

So why was he in the CIA's 8X, what was his destination, and why were his hands bound to the bedframe, and his head covered with a hood?

"Welcome back to the world of the awake," came a familiar voice.

"Okay, Hekka," he responded to his wife. "I understand the wrist restraints for those Serrano Indian S & M rituals you probably have planned, but the head gear is a bit much."

"The hood is necessary. Our destination is a surprise. From me to you. The tie downs? Marli says we're expecting—"

The aircraft suddenly plunged two hundred feet, twisting to starboard as pilot Marli Sommers fought the controls.

Crayle twisted and turned violently, his torso thrust up and forward. His secured wrists prevented him from being pitched about the jet's single bedroom like a three-point shot on a basketball court.

Hekka, who'd been standing nearby, hit the deck hard.

Crayle got himself back.

"You all right?"

Hekka moaned, then regained her feet after the plane leveled out. "As Marli says, any landing you can walk away from …"

"Cut me loose! Let me check you out!"

"You'll have plenty of time to check me out at our destination."

He felt a pinch on his bicep. He recognized the large needle feel of the CIA's Dial-A-Dose dormancy device. A glass cylinder filled with sleep-inducing fluid. With a dial atop for the number of minutes, or hours, the target was to remain unconscious. Clearly, it had been used on him back in the States. He'd no idea how long he'd been out, where they were, or his wife's intent.

Then, black.

Hekka replaced the drugging implement in its case.

Marli's voice came over the intercom. "That was a rough one. How's the passenger?"

"He's fine. He'd just come awake when we hit the turbulence. I sent him back into La-La-Land … for the duration."

"Good. Trust me. He'll thank you later."

"Right after his forgiveness for what I've done expresses itself."

Hekka heard the laugh in response. She pictured their boss's ex-wife fully in control of things on the flight deck up front, wearing her signature bright red lipstick, and those big, black-framed Hollywood sunglasses.

She shook her head, her enigmatic smile much in evidence.

• • •

Déjà vu all over again. Crayle woke up and felt around. He was lying on a bed of sorts, and he again heard the steady whoosh he recognized as characteristic of a French Dassault Falcon business jet.

Just then, the aircraft took a turbulence bump from the atmosphere. A bunk strap across his waist this time kept him from dumping onto the deck three feet below. And, he noticed, the hood was gone.

The door opened, and a dimmed lamp turned on.

In walked someone he recognized right away.

His wife, Hekka, attired in a French blue jump suit, removed the strap and coaxed him from the bed.

Her butterscotch skin was just part of her allure, but was just as beautiful each time he saw it.

"C'mon, sleepy head," she admonished. "Time for some breakfast. We'll be landing soon."

He followed her into the sumptuous cabin of CIA design.

After taking a seat, he noticed that all the window shades were drawn. He reached for the one nearest.

She intercepted his attempt.

"No. No. No," she admonished. "No hood. No window. The destination is a surprise, remember?"

He sort of did.

"Did you have sweet dreams, my darling?"

"Not exactly. It was that years ago op I did in Monaco."

"With Pattie Norbrunn."

"Yes. And Jack and Marli."

"The one that led to their divorce? After the lake incident in Zurich?"

"Yes. I kind of miss Marli with her bright red lipstick and Hollywood sunglasses."

"You're in luck. She's on the flight deck. Our pilot."

"Maybe she'll tell me where we're going."

"So, you're having dreams about Pattie. Should I be worried?"

"You mean after she tied me up and set fire to that room at the Versailles Palace? And you plopped in to save my sorry, captured ass by ramming your ten-inch Bowie knife clear through her heart? To the hilt?"

"I really hated to kill the new Queen of France on her inauguration day and all, but you needed her gone."

A familiar voice came over the intercom.

"We'll be down in fifteen. Buckle up."

No mention of the location.

CHAPTER 3

When they landed and deplaned, Hekka led her husband by the hand down a ramp and across the tarmac to a door. Since she'd replaced the black hood over his head, the guidance was necessary.

When a customs official started toward them, she threw up her hand with, "Back, please. He may have the newer version of that coronavirus. Very contagious."

Everyone backed away.

• • •

Standing on the tarmac, Hekka turned, waved goodbye to Marli, then placed her husband in a cab. She joined him and, a short ride later, carefully led him onto a boat.

"We're going to a very special place," she told him. "You'll like my surprise."

• • •

"Sitting on this particular beach in a couples lounge chair amid these grand rock pillars ..."

"Not exactly the Pillars of Hercules, but ... they'll do," said the butterscotch-toned beauty seated next to him.

"We'll save the Pillars of Hercules for another time. All we need—" His voice trailed off as he surveyed a figure approaching them from their left. A dwarf. Carrying a serving tray. With a bottle of champagne balanced on top.

Almost imperceptible, Crayle muttered, "Jack did this. Only he could pull off something like this. How far do we have to go to escape my employer?"

"The CIA?" Hekka pecked at her phone. "Nope. Trip Advisor says they can find us anywhere on the planet. It suggests we might try Mars when we get it colonized."

The dwarf, clad in a custom-fit tuxedo, arrived at the couple's side. "Good morning, Mr. and Mrs. Bond," he said with a distinctive French accent. "*Et bonjour. Comment ça va?*"

"*Ça va bien.*" Crayle waited a beat. "Let's see. Born in France in 1943. Suicide in 1993 at age 50. You're looking good for someone long dead, Nick Nack."

Crayle examined the bottle. "Mmm. Bollinger 1953. But I'm afraid you have the wrong spies. We are Mr. Magus and Mrs. Hekka Crayle. Not MI-6. CIA."

Crayle tilted his head back in order to address the satellite no doubt looming above. "Okay, Jack. You've had your fun. Now leave us with our champagne and kindly switch off the 'look down' features for what we intend to do on this beach after consuming said bubbly."

Hekka decided to play, as well. "Thank you, Nick Nack. That will be all for now. And please inform Mr. Scaramanga, we will not be available for the remainder of the day."

The suitably aged stand-in actor spun on his heel, retraced his path, and disappeared into the bushes.

"Look at that. Nick Nack left us no glasses," Crayle observed in an upper-class, British accent. "Drinking Bollinger '53 from the bottle … well, it's just not done."

Hekka popped the top to prove him wrong.

From there, they took turns with the champagne.

"This ocean is beautiful," she observed. "Is it the *Indian* Ocean?"

Crayle smiled. "I caught that. Sneaking in the 'Indian' thing again. I really must break you of that."

"That I am Serrano is indelible. It cannot be *broken*, as you say."

"Not everything is as it seems, my darling Indian person."

She lofted her left hand and, moving her head side-to-side, admired her wedding ring. "Person?"

"Wife, I meant."

"So …"

He glanced her way. "Any time a woman begins a sentence with '*So …*' a man knows he's in trouble. So, let's change the subject. Just look at the beauty of this ocean. Of course, sometimes we don't see what's below the surface."

"You're a spy. If you don't see beneath the surface, you die."

"Too true. Here, check this out." He fumbled a well-worn electronic device from the pocket of his trademark black cargo shorts.

"A little misdirection using the infamous CIA Universal Remote as bait?"

He let her remark slide. Said remotes had been utilized to trigger mini-nuclear devices around the world as well as for multitudinous other equally non-standard usages. They, however, did perform quite well in controlling TV sets. Upon selecting a new mode, and entering a numeric selection, he pressed the ***ENTER*** key.

Hekka turned toward a new sound. Something from the sea before them.

Several long thin poles rotated from below the surface. As they poked skyward, nets tethered between them came into view.

"Chinese fishing nets," Crayle explained.

The fishing aspect became clear when the nets seemed to come alive due to their abundant catch.

"That's something. And Chinese?"

"They have always had great influence in this part of the world. Notably, Singapore."

"Ling's new empire has quite some reach."

"She's up to it. Quite the world leader."

"And recently into her 20's. One has to be impressed."

Crayle clicked again, returning the nets to their operational submarine posture.

"Gotta keep those fish fresh," she concluded. "We'll be feasting on some of their predecessors later. Not far from here. In Phuket."

"Do they have a Hard Rock Café?"

"You know me too well."

"And that's just in the biblical sense."

They shared a laugh, then relaxed fully and drifted off to sleep.

• • •

A sound awakened them, and turned their attention back to the sea.

They noticed movement on the horizon.

A wide array of small power boats motored directly toward them.

Then, a man with a powered megaphone, standing on what appeared to be the lead boat, hollered, "Ahoy, Mr. Crayle!"

Mouths agape, their eyes panned the distance. Putting a positive, constructive interpretation just wasn't happening. The array of small water craft, side-by-side, continued its approach. Each bore several men armed with automatic weapons.

The man with the bullhorn in the center boat yelled orders right and left. "Fire for range. Either side. Do not hit them!"

His entourage executed his order, causing sand to kick up to either side of the Crayles' double-wide lounge chair.

The couple knew better than to move.

The leader spoke again. To them.

"Ahoy, Mr. Crayle. And Mrs. Crayle. We have you covered. Make no quick move."

He motioned to the boat on his right. It headed at top speed for the shore. "I'm afraid you are our prisoners," he gloated. "And with so little effort."

Crayle's finger activated the remote's ***REPEAT PRIOR*** function.

The Chinese fishing nets once more harvested their catch. Only this time, it was appended with the plethora of attack vessels. Including the one just dispatched to fetch the spy pair.

The spy turned to his wife. "Forget Bond … James Bond. How about Crayle … Mag Crayle?"

As soon as the attackers and their boats cleared the water, the sound of a jet aircraft invaded the scene from the Crayles' left. Slung low over the waves, it began to belch fire from a much-modified pitot tube.

"Micmac," the couple chorused.

The hundred rounds per second mini-gun shredded the water like a million voracious piranha.

The boats were transformed into toothpick rejects, and their occupants, inanimate seafood.

Seconds later, the jet banked into a 180-degree turn.

Crayle reached over. "Quick, Hekka!"

He grabbed her hand.

"Wrap your free hand around the lounge's arm rest!"

She did.

He punched in a new code on the CIA remote, then stuffed the device into a pocket.

A small weather balloon popped from the seat back, filled with helium, and deployed a hundred feet above them.

Somehow, the jet latched onto it and headed its catch across the water toward Phuket.

Crayle yelled at Hekka. "New book title!"

"Tell me!"

"*Withering Heights!*"

The two, on what would surely count as a Disney E-ticket, were delivered to a safe site adjacent to the world-renowned Thai resort city. As the jet approached at fifty feet, it disgorged the special lounge chair and occupants.

The assemblage hit the private runway at just North of the business jet's stall speed.

The lounge chair's runners had been specially designed to take the abuse. Fifty yards hence, the breathless Crayles slid to a stop.

• • •

One flight by Dassault Falcon, and two hours later, the Crayles arrived safely in Singapore.

CHAPTER 4

Back in the United States, at the covert STIF deep beneath the Manassas, Virginia battlefield park, spy Magus Crayle sat with American President Kimbel Stones.

"Where are you off to next?"

"You'd never guess."

"You're right. With all the intelligence resources I have at hand, you're still too good for me to track."

"Thanks for the accolade, Kimbel."

"Yeah. But let me try. How about … India?"

"How …"

The president formed a fist, glanced at his fingernails. "Sooner or later, it had to happen. Hekka is caught up in the Central Asia migrations thing."

"Nice deduction."

"No babysitting this time. Jack's more than busy serving as acting DCI."

"Flori and Marli love the babies."

"They are the two Strategic Solutions Office pilots. You'll need 'em."

"I was thinking of Susanna and Luisa."

"I can't win this, can I?"

"No, Mr. President. But look at the positive. I'll bring back some of that world-class Indian curry. I know you like hot stuff."

They were interrupted by a knock on the door. Susanna stepped in. "Jack Sommers is outside."

Stones waved, indicating she should show him in.

"So," Jack opened. "What's this about babysitting? Unless I can charge my Donald Trump rates ..."

"Which of his kids? Donald Junior?"

"Ivanka."

Jack Sommers' matter-of-fact delivery was subverted by a barely perceptible twitch at the corner of his lips.

"You've gone off to Fantasy Land, Jack. Look, we'll work something out for our baby. We'll be back in a couple of weeks. I'll spell you for a while at the Company. You can take a much-needed vacation, yourself."

"Yeah. Maybe Marli will take me back."

"You are indelibly married to Flori, and Marli would castrate your sorry ass if you made any kind of move on her ... or were ever other than indelibly committed to your marital relationship."

CHAPTER 5

No sooner had the president and Jack left the STIF, Hekka entered with Micmac in tow. Crayle turned first to his old friend and team associate.

"President Stones wants me now for that Director of Central Intelligence slot. I promised. I'll need a number two I can trust. I want you as DDCI, Micmac."

"Mag, you're the one. Consummate strategic planning skills. Cold NOC." He turned to Hekka. "Non-official cover. No stay-out-of-foreign-prison card like the pseudo-diplomats get." Then, back to Crayle. "Let's see. Operative skills. Tactical. Management. The whole schlemiel."

"Funny you ended with an homage to Lenny."

"He kind of sticks with you. But, you know, I miss the little guy."

Crayle knew all right. "France. Australia. He came through for us."

Micmac agreed. "Too bad we covert types never get recognition. No medals. No hurrahs."

"Did you ever ask for anything for your service?"

"No. I did what needed to be done, the best I could do it."

Hekka already knew she had a couple of good ones in her presence. But sadness lingered. "Lenny left behind a child. And Alona. Losing him really took her down. But she's tough. Back now doing her defense attorney thing in Big Bear. Making the judicial system work."

"Speaking of little guys, Micmac junior is growing up. Jack provided a fabulous nanny for him."

"Isn't she illegal?"

"Well, sorta. President Stones communications perfectionist, Luisa, the Brazilian, met her on a trip to the mother country. In Portugal. They became friends."

"Then your nanny is Portuguese?"

Micmac nodded.

Crayle grabbed the ensuing moment of silence. "Back on point?"

The former SEAL returned to the moment.

"Look. I'd love to help, Mag. But Ling, Empress of all that is China, needs me, too. Before I returned, I made her a promise similar to the one you gave Kimbel."

"The leader of the free world needs help. Ling needs help."

"You had time with her. You could go … "

Hekka reached into her oversized purse, and retrieved the large sharpening stone she used to hone her 10-inch Bowie knife. She regarded it as would a woman her nails, then glanced aside at the former SEAL.

"Belay my last," he said.

Crayle started to respond. His wife intervened.

"It means *disregard what I just said*. Phoebe keeps me up on Micmac's sailorisms."

The sailor in question smiled, and departed.

CHAPTER 6

Jack Sommers had just finished a brief Smartphone conversation. He stepped back into the STIF.

"Before you two go, I have something *Just In* … I always wanted to say that … from President Stones."

"I said we don't need anything. Just peace and quiet and our daughter."

"It's a trip. Expenses on the White House, via a proprietary, of course."

"Don't you think, Jack, after all that's come before in nearly every corner of the planet, that we might just be tripped out?"

"I'm afraid I have to insist."

A man and woman, who'd slipped in the door behind the Crayles, stepped close enough to inject them both.

They turned in their seats, tried to stand, and then slumped back as the drug won out.

The perpetrators of unconsciousness pressed hidden buttons on the chairs popping out small wheels, and carted them out of the STIF.

Jack called after them, "You'll thank me."

• • •

When the Crayles woke hours later, they found themselves side by side and strapped to a bed. This time there were no hoods over either of their heads.

Standing next to them, pilot Marli said, "Leave the strap alone. It's more than secure. And the flesh tone patches on your shoulders each have a tiny circuit inside. I press certain keys on my CIA Universal Remote, and you get even more restful sleep."

"Where to this time?" Crayle wanted to know.

"We'll behave," Hekka added.

Marli looked from respondent Hekka to the one most likely to cause trouble.

"She'll see that I behave," said Crayle. "She has that female gene."

Marli touched her thumb, and its print, to the buckle, and thus unfastened the restraining strap.

She headed back to the flight deck.

Minutes later Marli's familiar admonition piped over the intercom.

"We'll be down in fifteen. Buckle up!"

The minutes ticked off like eons. Until they reached fifteen.

The jet's cabin came alive.

"Touchdown!"

Crayle checked the flat panel TV screen for a football game. Then, he realized it was the intercom.

"Ten minutes!"

The Crayles buckled up. They truly missed Kianna. Surely Jack would get them back to Washington, D.C. quickly. From there, back home. To Big Bear. To their cabin.

Marli landed the jet light as a feather. Soon after, its contents stood on the tarmac with luggage being piled into a black limo.

With the airport residing on Singapore's East side, the ride was a long, visual-filled trip across town to the city's storied port.

On the way, the couple spotted the iconic Marina Bay Sands—a three acre surfboard with bar and infinity pool—propped atop three 56-story skyscrapers that served as guest rooms.

They turned to each other.

"We'll stay there someday," they chorused.

Arriving at the port, they were personally escorted aboard the 2,184 passenger cruise ship, the Celebrity Constellation.

CHAPTER 7

This wasn't their first cruise ship. And they weren't typical passengers.

The Celebrity Constellation appeared to validate the statistics Crayle gleaned from his Smartphone on the way from Singapore's Changi Airport. The vessel extended 965 feet in length, with a 105.6 foot beam, its widest point. Beyond the numbers, it was just beautiful.

The 24 knot cruising speed sounded like a bonus. And the Crayles were in no hurry.

Showing their special passports, they were introduced to a man who would zip them through registration and facilitate the transport of their luggage. He led them up the gangway to the elevators.

As was their nature, Magus and Hekka Crayle observed every detail along the way. No one noticed them any more than normal.

Instead of the usual mid-ship elevators, which remained quite busy during normal embarkation hours, their assigned concierge led them forward to one especially for them.

A short ride, and they entered their suite.

Crayle stepped to a desk, and hefted the champagne bucket there. "Just the right amount." He plucked the bottle, and read, "Dom Perignon '57. I wonder if Jack would mind if we used this for mimosas?"

The concierge blanched, as if a heart attack would soon follow. "You are kidding, Mr. Crayle, aren't you?"

He smiled over at the man, then glanced around. "Now, where are the plastic cups?"

The concierge embraced his right elbow with his left hand, and used the free one to massage his Van Dyke goatee. And said no more.

He left with a nice tip.

Thirty minutes later, the Crayles relaxed on their roomy balcony, now on their third glass of Dom. In lead crystal champagne flutes delivered post haste on the orders of their concierge.

There it was again. In the not far distance, the Marina Bay Sands hotel.

Crayle began a list of its accoutrements. "Convention center. Gambling casino. Shops."

"And Raffles Hotel, with its famous Singapore Sling, not far away."

"Yes," said Crayle. "We can see what effect the Slings have on Serrano Indians."

"Ooh. Slings plural."

"You bet."

"Mr. Crayle, I propose a toast."

He raised his glass. A light refracted through into his eyes. He squinted them shut.

"Don't tear up just yet," she said.

"It was the light. I saw the light."

She knew what he meant, but stayed in her part.

"May the good you *see* today be exceeded by the good you *do* tomorrow."

They clinked glasses.

"I'd replace *exceeded* with *surpassed*."

"So, now I've got an editor," she teased back.

Now, it was his turn.

"And may the love that I made to you yesterday be surpassed by the love that I make to you … in about fifteen minutes."

They toasted.

More robustly, this time.

• • •

Later, in their stateroom, and post some world-class lovemaking, they sat naked on the balcony.

Pushing into late Fall in this part of the world didn't change things much. The evenings were still warm and, with the typical ambient humidity, balmy.

Hekka reached to her side and clasped her husband's hand.

"Ah, yes. You got me off program in there." He nodded back at the room.

"Channel Darryl then," she insisted.

"Our famous or otherwise covert travel agent provided our itinerary. Replete with a few don'ts. Like, when our ship docks tomorrow at Phuket, on its way West, don't get off. Don't even show ourselves."

"Too bad. I so wanted to visit James Bond Island again. From a ship's perspective, I believe that would be called an excursion."

"When they write them up, they tell passengers MILD, MODERATE, or STRENUOUS. I'm not sure they have the EXTREME that would apply."

"Go on."

"Next, Sri Lanka. Stay aboard, he said. The Tamils may revolt again."

"Noted. Next."

"We'll make port in Mumbai. The old Bombay. Darryl's set us up for an excursion there that's of the MILD category. No bullets, bombs, or blades."

"I don't know. We'll have been on the ship so long by then, we may go ashore and act like sailors."

"That reminds me. I need to give Micmac a call one of these days."

"The champagne is having its way with me, but I think I recall him wanting to go help Empress Ling over there in Hong Kong."

"Well, if I call and he's gone dark, we can conclude that's where he is."

"Write yourself a note."

"Let's go back inside. I'm feeling naked out here."

Hekka smiled.

"You are."

• • •

Having docked the next morning, Crayle awakened to a firm rapping on the stateroom door. He rubbed the sleep from his eyes. After padding to and pulling it open, in stepped the bearer of his near-term dream. Breakfast comprised of eggs over medium, crisp bacon, English muffins with marmalade, and a pot of decaf coffee.

After the delivery man departed, Crayle stepped to the bed and gave Hekka a mild shake.

She mimicked the eye rub, and her sense of smell instantly engaged.

They enjoyed the repast.

Finished, he needed a couple of documents from the room safe. He tried four digits. Month and day of birth. No. Ah. In foreign sequence. Day and month of birth. No luck. Phone code, ATM code. No go. One left to try. The last four digits of his fake social security number. There.

He extracted wallets and passports, and checked the wallets. Money and cards there.

Money in foreign currency plus U.S. dollars.

Check.

Passports replete with India sticker in both plus the requisite Landing Permits for Mumbai.

Done.

Last, he located the two slips of paper that would allow them to board the correct ground transportation for their chosen tour.

• • •

By 9 a.m., the pair was off on their first excursion of the cruise. Magus and Hekka Crayle soon proceeded down the gangway, through the terminal welcoming them, in large letters, to Mumbai, and into their awaiting tour bus.

The culmination of the Mumbai Grand Tour followed with a trip down Marine Drive, and beautiful bay views. Next, a stop to see the impressive Gateway of India arch, which welcomed arrivals from the long ago to today. And, no doubt, well beyond. After that, they paused for photos of the grand Victoria Gothic styled railway station. Crayle took a shot at its name.

"Well done," Hekka applauded. "That sounded a lot like the *Chhatrapati Shivaji Maharaj Terminus*," she said, with a perfect mimic of robot Number 5 from the movie, Short Circuit.

"How'd you do that?"

"I'll never tell. In fact, it's one of many secrets I'll never tell."

"You know what? You're a tease."

Finally, they arrived at the illustrious and quite famous Taj Mahal Palace Hotel. It was known as one of Asia's top hotels, with Moorish columns, arches, and red domes. The beauty didn't end outside.

Post security and forehead temperature checks, the tourists trouped inside through a sumptuous, marble everywhere lobby. The inlays and columns provided the feel of the old British-influenced era.

Crayle noticed a large seating area to their left as they marched by. Beyond it, probably the most splendiferous of registration desks he'd ever seen. Perhaps, some time to explore after the promised hors d'hoeuvres and a sampling of India's Kingfisher beer.

And so it came to pass. After the repast and imbibing, the two scouted the ground floor for about twenty minutes. The high-end shops. The famous majestic stairway.

Crayle hugged his wife. "Let's do the Kama Sutra thing. Right here."

In response, he received her minimalist Serrano Indian smile. "Come. Let's inform our guide that we're leaving the tour. We're going for a walk."

CHAPTER 8

There they were. Early evening walking hand-in-hand on Mumbai's renowned seaside promenade between the beautiful beach and likewise famous Marine Drive. The feel was balmy and not too humid. Near perfect.

Magus Crayle nudged his wife's lips with his own. It felt good. She nudged back.

"I suspect you have the evening planned out. In excruciating detail."

"Not sure about excruciating, but let's just enjoy the moment."

"Yes. Walking down Mumbai's seaside promenade."

"We'll pretend we're alone. Like that time in Portugal."

"Estoril, I believe it was called. One-time home to Ian Fleming, as well as his Casino Royale inspiration."

"You know your spy thriller writers, don't you?"

"Only one in the biblical sense."

So easy to smile now. No bullets. No blades. No bombs.

He peered into her eyes. "Let's pretend we're alone."

"Ignore the million or so folks all up and down this walkway?"

"Like Estoril. Let's get naked and make sweet, beautiful love on the beach."

"Public displays of affection aren't allowed in this part of the world."

"That's just the Muslim part. Here in India, it's okay. Kama Sutra, and all."

"You're going to introduce me to that … here on the beach?"

"Hmmm. *Love On The Beach.* As a title. I might just start writing romance novels."

"You could begin them all with a momentous event. Like ours. At the Tack Store. In Big Bear."

"Where men tried to murder you?"

"Yeah. Get the blood flowing."

"I'll give your idea some thought."

He noticed each time he took his eyes off her, and glanced about, all who saw Hekka became transfixed by her beauty. The combination of her father's reddish brown skin tone and her mother's pale white Finnish rendition had produced a hue resembling butterscotch. Together with the silky, waist length, black hair, and the gold trimmed, ruby red Sari, they couldn't allow their eyes to disengage.

"What about Jack? We haven't heard from him for days now. That's not like him."

"I engaged the OTG button on my Smartphone. Off-The-Grid."

"He's saved our lives more than once."

"He who leadeth you into the valley of the shadow of death, has to get you the hell out."

"You're just full of biblical knowledge."

"Remind me to ask my mother when we return home. What manner of sweet, innocent choir boy became Crayle One, Two, and Three?"

"That has to be classified information. Say, I wonder what Jack's doing right now."

"He's busy twenty-four seven running the Strategic Solutions Office off books ops. The Office of Specialized Staffs above that. And the entire CIA above that. Hands full."

"Interesting. So what's the question, right now, Mag, that's at the top?"

"Why didn't they kill me at Phuket?"

"Now there's a mystery."

"All those boats with guns blazing, and no hits. It implies they wanted to scare us—which I doubt—or push us somewhere else."

She was puzzled. "To India? How would they know we'd come here?"

He gave it a moment. "Your research on migrations of the so-called indigenous is known to the public. They know you're hot on the trail of a link between the Asian subcontinent residents, and those peoples who migrated from the Lena River region northeast across Siberia into Alaska. And down."

"From public knowledge to an armed assault. Now that's a stretch."

"Machine guns? I've had a few tough critics, but ..."

"I bet Langley or Manassas will pick up something."

"Jack should be checking that out in his spare time. He'll let us know if he turns up something." He changed the subject, and pointed. "You see those high, spherical, white street lights over there on Marine Drive? Viewed from above, they appear like a luminous string of pearls. The Queen's Necklace, they're called."

She turned back to him. "How are you feeling?"

"It's a bit unnerving with all these people here on the promenade."

Hekka gave him a thoughtful glance. "Your suffering from Custer's syndrome."

"What?"

"General George Armstrong Custer."

"What's he got to do with this crowd?"

"Take another look around."

He did.

"You're surrounded by Indians."

CHAPTER 9

The Crayles continued to the end of the Mumbai promenade, passing a wide crescent of beautiful beach before they paused in front of a centuries-old building.

Surprised by a door opening right next to him, Crayle braced for a fight with a defensive stance.

A frail man in his thirties, wearing a disheveled khaki shirt over dark brown trousers, held up his hands. He appeared harmless.

"Can I help you?"

The man shook his head. No English.

He stumbled backwards a couple of steps and Crayle moved to stop the closing, spring-loaded door from hitting the man.

Unphased by the event, Hekka decided to use the moment. "You do the Good Samaritan, I'm going over there to that rack of beautiful Saris. Let me know when you're done." She headed away toward the referenced, makeshift, street-side shop.

The man, suddenly strong as an ox, grabbed Crayle's wrists and yanked him inside. And pulled a revolver from behind his back.

The door slammed.

Crayle assumed a robbery, and spoke first.

"How'd you select us?"

The gunman tilted his chin. "The camera around the neck. Expensive lens. Tourists with money."

Crayle looked down at the camera. "Try out my new creation on your trip," Micmac had requested. After hearing the specifics, Crayle added, "For Science and Technology? At Langley?"

That was then. Now it made him a target.

"I've not used it yet. Let me get a shot of you."

A book dropped out of Crayle's bag. The back flipped open, revealing the author bio, and a head and shoulders photo of the author.

The gunman glanced down. "That's you." He looked back and forth to verify his conclusion. "Magus Crayle. Hey, take one of me, just like that one."

"You want me to have your picture?"

"I'll take the camera when we are done."

"You want a headshot?"

"I know that's what you call them. I read a lot. Yes, a headshot."

Crayle stepped back, lifted the camera, and focused the lens. He held the device firm, sighted the subject, and pressed the button.

The discharge inside recoiled the camera. The .38 Special slug blew through the thousand-dollar lens striking the gunman square in the forehead. That power, from a few feet distant, slammed the gunman to the ground.

Special components within the lens served to mute the report. No one outside the room heard a thing.

Crayle stepped back outside.

He turned to Hekka. "You all right?"

"I'm fine. Look what I bought." She held up a garment in a bright blue with gold overlays. She nodded toward the now closed door. "What was with your wounded Indian?"

"He saw my fancy camera. Wanted a headshot."

While they talked, the woman with the Sari shop approached them. "I'm sorry about that. But there will be ten more like him unless you come with me."

Crayle was a little more than perplexed. "Ten more? Come with you?"

"Someone wishes to meet you. Someone very special."

"I didn't like the first greeting. Why should I …"

She pointed behind them. "Just over there. Where the wealth lives."

The Crayles turned their gaze to where the lady indicated. Yes, they saw some quite grand villas just a couple of blocks distant.

He turned to Hekka. "Well, nothing like an adventure."

"Come," the woman said. "I'll lead you there. To your adventure."

CHAPTER 10

Fifteen minutes later, Crayle and Hekka found themselves in a sumptuous residence in a South Mumbai area replete with high-end abodes. In a living room of ornate accoutrements, they sat across from their host, who'd introduced himself as Rustom 'Rusty' Modi.

Just then, the door opened and a woman, approximately 5'7" and with flesh tone slightly lighter than the man before them, entered. She raised her hand as Rusty began to speak. "I will introduce myself. I'm Leonor. Rusty's wife."

"Not from here by your name."

"No. Not Mumbai. A distance south of here. Goa. Originally a Portuguese colony. Though born in India, those are my roots."

Crayle thought briefly of the two ethnic Portuguese women now in America's White House. He'd the same sense of them each time they'd entered the room.

Luisa who'd moved from proofreader at The San Ernestino Observer newspaper in Southern California to President Kimbel Stones' side, to ensure a clean, concise message in his communications. In the

West Wing, everyone stopped what they were doing whenever she came into view.

Then, Flori. The other Brazilian beauty who now flew covert spy ops via specially prepared business jets for Jack Sommers' Strategic Solutions Office, SSO. From this woman's demeanor alone, Crayle could tell she'd fit right in with Luisa and Flori.

Hekka's eyes poured over their host's wife. She appeared an enigma. She had the dark hair of the Indian females Hekka witnessed on the promenade, but the tone was off somehow. She was sensitive due to her own unique coloration. And the black hair. Not the straight beautiful streams, but rather pin curls, each the size of a quarter, tight to her head. Her figure would attract just about any man, but could indeed fill out in her latter years. Hekka felt a curiosity about the woman. The man interrupted her meanderings.

"They say, Mr. Crayle, that one should never bring up the topics of religion or politics. I find them both fascinating. Don't you agree?"

Crayle knew the fascination well. He nodded.

At that thought, the wife stood and stretched out her hand to Hekka. "That was the man talk signal. I know it well. Come, my darling guest. We'll go shopping."

Hekka turned to her husband.

"We'll be fine," he said.

The two women were out the door and piling into a pink Mercedes. One with Iranian plates.

"We have a wonderful department store. *Carrefour*. It's French."

"I know the name. We get around a lot. But no. Take me to a Hard Rock Café, if you have one."

"The lady knows what she wants." She leaned over and slid her hand up Hekka's thigh. And stopped. What's this?"

"It's my ten-inch Bowie knife. American women carry them to ward off poachers."

The hand was removed.

"Buckle up. We're an hour or two south of Andheri West. Why the Hard Rock?"

"I pick up black T-shirts for Magus and our good friend, Micmac. The latter is a musician, among other things." She didn't elaborate about the former SEAL and gadget creator for the CIA's Science and Technology Directorate.

"You'll want to get out your Smartphone."

"Why's that?"

"Capture a video along the way."

She started the car and moved out onto the street. "Disney should have this ride."

"For the sights? Like Main Street?"

"E-ticket!"

The rationale for the characterization quickly became evident.

CHAPTER 11

Crayle continued the dialog. "So, religion and politics. I believe you, as my host, should go first."

The host fetched a pair of crystal *old fashioned* glasses plus a new bottle of a favorite South Asian liquor. *Officer's Choice Black. Exquisite and Rare*, the label proclaimed. The displaced Persian, in India referred to as a Parsi, filled them to the top.

Crayle anticipated a long discussion.

"Zoroastrianism dates back to the Persian Empire. The Arab conquest and consequent persecutions drove most followers away. Many came to Mumbai."

"So your roots go back to pre-Iran. Are you Zoroastrian?"

"I am. But we are a dwindling lot. Marriage and procreation are at all time lows."

"I know Christianity, Judaism, and Islam, as well as the Eastern religions. Give me a thumbnail version of Zoroastrianism."

"To be concise, it describes the eternal battle between good and evil. And that individuals have to choose between them."

"Is there some mysticism mixed in?"

"Yes. The notion of magic emanates from my religion. In fact, your very given name derives from it. Magus. You are the Magic Man."

Crayle smiled. His host had his CIA code name right there, and didn't realize it.

CHAPTER 12

It was amazing. The traffic in Mumbai moved along at a pace slightly faster than the Los Angeles 405 at rush hour. The trucks and busses tended to stay in their lanes, but taxis and other cars darted into the tiniest of ample space. Weaving in and out of the four-wheeled traffic were the motorbikes and scooters. Weaving in and out of that mélange were pedestrians, transiting at random from one side of the road to the other. All the mayhem and chaos took place in real time.

Hekka captured it all on her CIA issue phone. Magus wouldn't believe this without the video. She wondered, how many of these people die each day?

The wife read her thoughts. "They all know the game so well that there are few fatalities."

Holding the phone for a steady view out the front, Hekka caught the visual enigma out the side window. Modern buildings, some of them sky scrapers, interspersed with segments of color-rich shanties. The latter seemed placed randomly aside and atop one another and appeared vulnerable to any manner of strong wind or monsoon-like storms.

"They are approximately three meters by three meters square—nine feet by nine feet in your measure—and can house ten people."

"These are the poor, then."

"Poor is pocket book, rich is heart."

Hekka spotted a mosque off to the left, accessible by a low tide causeway. Worshippers lined up from its front entrance all the way to the mainland.

"It's the Haj Ali Mosque."

They proceeded over a tall, long bridge over the eastern extreme of the Arabian Sea, then slowed through a segment of road construction. Without warning, the wife zipped to the right, up an alley, stopping in front of the Hard Rock Café, Mumbai.

Inside, Hekka ordered a hot fudge milk shake, along with two shots of whiskey, which she dumped in the shake.

"I'll have one of those," said the wife.

"You're driving."

"Here in India, we know about walking and chewing gum."

She was right, Hekka reasoned. It was clear everyone on the thoroughfares wanted to get from their personal A's to their personal B's. Life incarnate.

They proceeded on with food orders. Hekka had the Buffalo Style Sliders, three, and her host, the Whiskey Bacon Java Sliders with Jack Daniels supplying the sweetener. Also, a trio.

Finished Hekka asked the waitress for T-shirts.

"I'm sorry, ladies. We're out of T-shirts."

"I've come half way around the world. Could you please check in back."

The waitress huffed away.

As if on cue, the house system began a song that said a lot, just in its title. It was true. She and husband Mag always seemed like they were arriving at the *Crossroads*.

The waitress returned holding three shirts. "Only these. They're *Grande* in the French parlance, XL in American."

"Perfect," Hekka responded. "Give me all three."

She turned to her companion. "One each for Magus and Micmac, and one for me. I like to sleep in them."

The wife smiled. "You don't worry about staining them?"

"My husband is quite accurate."

CHAPTER 13

Mick MacKay, known to his team members as Micmac, had landed here before, but in the company of the team. Chek Lap Kok, otherwise known as Hong Kong International, sat on a just-large-enough island on the north side of, and attached by bridge to, the much larger Lantau Island. All of that, West of Hong Kong Island. For an armored stretch limo, the black, generic appearance allowed Micmac to take on the air of a visiting diplomat, versus the royal purple Imperial stretch that was Empress Ling's personal ride and brought major attention of the press to identify its occupants.

The somewhat circuitous route to Empress Ling's palace perched atop Hong Kong Island appeared on a map similar to a bulge-up parenthesis laid on its side. Travel time from airport to palace clocked in at a little under one hour. Under normal conditions, not bad.

Hong Kong, its waters, and Kowloon retained their beauty regardless of season, or even time of day.

Once up the hill, concern came over Micmac's countenance as the route normally taken through the Central District moved a little West. The street names he observed, such as Garden Road and

Cotton Tree Drive, would seem better suited to the American Mid-West or South. The driver, ever checking his rearview mirror, read the trepidation.

"There is construction in Central. We … circumvent problem." He seemed pleased with his ability to nail a sophisticated word in English.

Micmac noted the current street appeared to head away, then back toward the peak. He noted a grand building that once housed a military hospital. Hmm. Bowen Road. He wondered what the eponymous individual had accomplished to be so honored. If he did good on his current mission, perhaps he'd get a MacKay Road.

Inside the palace compound, he was led by a crew of security personnel inside to the private quarters of the empress.

"Hello, Mr. Micmac. It's been a while. As I told Magus … Mr. Crayle … I need help. Help I can trust."

"People who trust each other best communicate using first names. Magus is fine with that. So am I. You?"

"Magus and Micmac, then. Please, call me Annie."

The tall, colorful, majestic curtains at the far end of the room parted.

Micmac slid his hand to the pistol secluded at the small of his back. He'd heard about the attempted poisoning of Ling and that the prime suspect was Yellow. When the young empress showed no signs of worry, he relaxed.

Yellow placed a tray before them, then hefted the ancient teapot, and did the unexpected. She poured a small portion into a nearby fish tank. The three observed.

After approximately two minutes, and with no fish heeling over dead, Yellow poured two cups.

"If you don't mind, I'm having Yellow join us, hence the additional cup."

Micmac nodded. He observed that Ling was still learning her new position. Empresses didn't need to ask permission. For anything.

He also observed there was a fourth cup and saucer. "Your successor would be Yellow, or White. Am I correct?"

"You are as bright as Magus said."

The curtains parted once more. In walked a very pregnant White daughter. She took the final seat, and filled the remaining cup with tea.

"So, Annie, what's up that you requested our help?"

The two of Chin's adopted daughters took note of the familiarity he'd used.

"Before I married my adoptive father, and even before he replaced the former government, they had a very sophisticated network for spying on interesting parties around the globe."

"Yes. But they did not use that ugly word, stealing. Their communism was a belief that everything belongs to everyone. That the world is at its best as one giant commune."

"A quite convenient set up for those in charge."

"As you know, it's a belief system."

"In the extreme."

"Yes. The lesser true believers in the system are fanatical about it. All enemies and detractors must be eliminated."

"Magus once characterized it. No one owns anything so that everyone can own everything."

"He shared that with me as he helped father overthrow those people. With his Blackstone Strategy."

"He also said there is always an elite group at the top. They use the fanatics for their dirty work. He reasoned that the leaders were not necessarily believers at all, but saw the extreme ideology as an excuse to claim absolute power over the masses."

"History bears that out. But how does the long, multipronged reach of the previous regime bring us together?"

"It's the oil. That reach continues and extends to many countries."

"But why? Your father, and late husband, managed the new empire into a free enterprise one. No need to be sneaky. No need to prop up a failed ideology."

"For those involved, old habits die very, very hard."

"If I read this right, the legitimate power is vested in the Empress of China. You. The rule of one. But you have discovered an oligarchy not far beneath the surface of the previous China. Rule by the several."

"Both cannot continue. The people deserve a clean hierarchy. My total commitment is to them. The oligarchs only commit to themselves."

"So, a tug of war regarding benefits to the masses."

"This is almost like talking to Magus. You are quite perceptive."

"Hanging around with Mag—it rubs off."

Micmac noticed Yellow and White daughters trying to appear nonchalant. He knew they were taking in every word. But, for whom? And Ling never did anything except by design. The presence of the other two was not social.

Ling finished her tea. "We do more serious talk later this evening. Right now, we're all headed out. Party time!"

The nascent empress's youth bore through. She sounded just like twenty-year-olds around the globe.

CHAPTER 14

Rustom Modi and Magus Crayle continued their conversation unabated. The liquor was holding out, and both seemed interested in each others point of view, especially when it varied from their own. It was clear, though, to Crayle that the Parsi didn't have him there to delve deeper into the realm of the Zoroastrian religion. He knew something far more present and serious was likely in the offing. The Parsi didn't disappoint.

"It appears, Mr. Crayle, you've removed the means of achieving our near-term goals. Destroying the covert nuclear weapons factory in China and taking out the primary scientists all at once. As you are aware from your own voluminous spy activities, secrets such as mini-nuke design and creation are supremely compartmented."

"I truly hate destroying dreams, Rusty. Especially those of megalomaniacs."

"We have three of the devices … here."

This was the substance Crayle knew was coming. He just hadn't expected it to come so straightforward, and easily. It gave him pause. If a captor, which the Parsi had positioned himself to be, let on critical information, it could well indicate the listener was not expected to survive to tell. The Parsi continued.

"The rest are secreted where neither you nor any of your ilk can discover them."

"Those would be the other three. Of the six total."

"I typically appreciate a well-informed intellectual, Mr. Crayle. Not as much for a spy."

"Understood. I'll try and disappoint you further. Since you immediately began right away to out yourself as Illuminé, you must be quite confident I won't be able to pass on that juicy piece of intel."

"And I am truly sorry for that circumstance."

• • •

The Parsi excused himself to eliminate excess fluids.

Alone, Crayle had a moment to reflect on the quite serious circumstance.

His first notion was to locate and destroy, or confiscate, the nuclear devices somehow. To that end, he'd have to learn their locations, free himself from Modi, and proceed from there.

Given the circumstance, and with Hekka away and unaware of the forming risks, he'd have to be more clever this time than at any time in the past.

It hit him. Like a figurative ton of bricks.

He would play along. Make Modi believe he absolutely needed the strategic spy master to realize his goals.

Now what, he wondered, was he, Magus Crayle, able to offer beyond his sophisticated planning expertise.

He closed his eyes. A picture formed in his mind.

He had it.

Access.

To President Stones.

CHAPTER 15

The ride from the palace down from Victoria Peak produced the usual post card views. As the sun finished its descent to the West, it provided last light to the natural and concocted grandeur that was Hong Kong. The metropolis below, which stretched along the coast to North Point, and beyond. Victoria Harbour with its boats. Kowloon on the far side followed by the rest, known for quite a few decades as the New Territories. The lights of Shenzhen just coming to life on the northern horizon. Micmac checked left on a China Eastern airliner heading out from Hong Kong International. And then the international gambling epicenter, Macau, an hour's ferry ride from Hong Kong Island. Beauty everywhere.

"All the road work we circumvented coming in seems to have stopped. Do they take up everything but the barricades each day at dusk?"

Ling smiled. She gave him a particularly long glance. He felt it. She felt it. Yet another complication.

Quickly, he moved on. "You set that up. The road work was fake. It allowed us to have this normally busy road to ourselves. And to keep people a distance from your purple limo. Now, I feel special."

He gave it a moment. Ooh, he thought. This is beginning to act like a date.

They reached their destination ten minutes later. Outside, he saw the sign. ***HARD ROCK CAFÉ***.

The staff at the Hard Rock, like all of China and the rest of the world, knew what Empress Ling looked like. The crew at The Rock, as they liked to call it, also knew that, when she arrived in street garb along with friends so attired, she was to go 'unrecognized' and be treated just the same as 'any other' patron. Right.

Ling's timing was, as usual, perfect. Two minutes after they were seated and had ordered drinks, the entertainers entered onto their performance platform, bowed to their fans, and cranked up some classic rock and roll. After the first number, a waiter passed a note to the leader. He didn't need a note to know that the empress was in attendance. What he saw caused him to smile. Her honored guest had something in common with the musicians. He was, among other things, one of them.

Micmac joined the band onstage. Their leader's English was excellent. He seemed to know a lot more than he should. He handed the former SEAL, and current spy, a guitar. A Les Paul Custom with mahogany sides and back, a carved maple top, and a maple fretboard. Just like his at home. After a brief whispered discussion, they settled on one that all knew. And that seemed somehow appropriate for the occasion. An old Doobie Brothers hit. *China Grove*.

Ling ogled Micmac as did many others. She wondered aloud, "Why American men always wore those tight trousers."

The band finished their first number to a great deal of applause, and the leader spoke into his microphone in excellent, unaccented English.

"Thank you very much." He gave a brief bow. "Just one more with Mr. Micmac. One he picked himself. A song by a great American Classic Rock legend, Mr. Johnny Rivers."

Micmac had to smile deeply in consideration of his Crayle team members, living and deceased, as he counted the band into a Hong Kong rendition of *Secret Agent Man*.

When they'd finished, there was plenty of applause. A standing O. Micmac bowed deeply to the audience and to his impromptu band mates. He took off the guitar to hand it back.

"No," said the leader. "Yours to keep. A souvenir."

Yes, he thought. A three to five thousand dollar souvenir.

One look at Ling and he knew who'd set that up. Nice.

He descended the stage, walked to where Ling sat, and laid his new instrument on the table for all to see up close. He pulled a felt marking pen from his hip pocket. "I want your autograph," he said to Ling.

A quizzical look later, she asked, "How do you want it?"

A pregnant pause. "Right here in Chinese characters. Mag called them Sinograms."

She signed. "And ... "

"Underneath: Annie in English writing. Beneath that, Empress Of All That Is China."

"There won't be any room left for any other autographs."

He looked deep into her eyes. "I won't be wanting any more."

They had several more drinks apiece before returning to the palace. Now, free to express their feelings and their passions, he walked her to her door, and inside.

She turned to him, eyes locked, and disrobed. Her hands flew up to cup his face, and she planted a long, deep kiss on his lips. Slowly, he pulled back.

"Annie. You're single. The most eligible female on the planet. I ... I'm still in mourning. For my late wife."

"I can do the other for you. As a place holder. For when you have let her go."

"You are beyond beautiful, Annie. I now can see what Mag faced when he was here, and you were just sixteen. I have to say no. For now."

As he walked the seeming endless distance to his room, the sailor in him admonished, but the man who'd loved Phoebe with all of his being knew he'd done right.

CHAPTER 16

Hekka Crayle continued to relax with Parsi Rustom Modi's wife, Leonor, in Mumbai's Hard Rock Café. Her curiosity came to the fore. And her desire to later relate intel, actionable or not, to her husband when they were alone.

"If you don't mind, I'd like to hear about you. And about your husband. I find you interesting, separately, and as a couple."

"There is a lot to tell. Perhaps …"

"Please?" Hekka got the waitress's attention, and pointed to her empty glass. A little more sign language, and the woman headed off to fetch another special shake. She turned back to her host.

"I'll start with me. I, too, am a blend of two ethnicities. Portuguese. Indian. The former from my father. He had business in the Velha Goa, and he met someone there. They married. She got pregnant."

"You?"

She nodded. "My mother was quite religious. She adopted my father's Roman Catholicism and attended the Basilica do Bom Jesus in Old Goa."

"Let me guess. The Basilica of Good Jesus."

"Yes. The priest was very emotional, a common Portuguese trait, and addressed his flock in loud, evocative sermons. One Sunday, my mother responded in loud outcries of her own."

"She was very religious, like your husband."

"That, too. This time, she'd gone into labor."

"Oh!"

"Her words exactly."

"Let me guess, you were born right then and there in the Basilica."

"I was. The priest only lost his audience and momentum for a couple of minutes. Then, at the top of his lungs, he proclaimed, '*It's a miracle!*'"

Hekka drew a brief smile. "Sometimes it's difficult for clerical types to yield the stage. I hope your mother didn't take offense."

"She was busy with other things. It's just as well. He would be the one to baptize me, and would later claim to have 'delivered' both of us."

"So, an Indian mother, Portuguese father. How did he get to India in the first place. And why?"

Hekka knew from her spy tradecraft that people become more forthcoming as they loosened. Leonor appeared to be well down the road. She could deliver precious intel regarding her husband, the real person of interest.

"In the Sixteenth Century, the Portuguese traders and colonists arrived and conquered Old Goa from the Adil Shahi Dynasty, it is said. Goa became not only a trading port, but also the focal point for the Christianization in this part of the world. All Christian sects were based there. Then, the epidemics. Cholera. Malaria. The devastation decimated the large population. To a hundredth of its former self. Just over two thousand today."

"And the man who proclaimed you a miracle?"

"He lives. Still the Patriarch of the basilica."

"Patriarch?" Hekka's backstory was of an indigenous religious upbringing. Of her father's Serrano heritage. Her Finnish mother had no trouble embracing its teachings.

"Yes. Such as is the case with Venice and Lisbon, my father's home town. A suburb, actually. Interestingly, Patriarchs take direction directly from the Pope."

Hekka sat back. She wasn't going to mention that the previous Pope, blown to Heaven by Pattie's mini-nuclear device, turned out to be a member of a very secret, global society. And that all members' religious zeal directed itself toward the enlightened. Or, in French, the Illuminé. As such, they eschewed God-centered beliefs, and swore themselves to atheism as if they would one day become the collective god.

"Your father? Is he still alive?"

"Yes. He lives in his ancestral home just outside of Lisbon. It's a grand place. Once occupied by the King of Portugal."

"I've been to Estoril. At the seaside next to Lisbon. Also the writing habitat of the James Bond series author. Ian Fleming."

"No. His is in a different area."

Hekka put it together. His ancestral home had belonged to a king. Her father was royal blood. She thought of the late Sylvain Lalumière. His quest to reinstate the French monarchy via miniaturized nuclear devices, made in China, had actually worked. He'd been Illuminé. And his death on his coronation day, at Pattie's hand, had put his son, Jean-Marc, in the top spot. King Louis XX.

"Your father, like your mother, is deeply religious?"

"Please don't repeat this. But, no. It is a pretense. Organized religion disgusts him. The tremendous wealth of the church leaves many millions of poverty-stricken people in its wake. He believes that only the intellectual mind can lead to solutions."

"He would get on well with Magus. He, too, has a great mind." She considered their potential to become very serious adversaries. She wondered how her husband was getting along with the Parsi host.

CHAPTER 17

Crayle continued to engage the Mumbai Parsi. His own CIA background demanded as much.

"What of your heritage? I sense there's something you want more than anything. Please …"

The Parsi waxed quite serious. His eyes peered into the distance, only confined by the wall opposite.

"Simply put, I want the return of Persia. So I, and the other Parsis, can return. For that, the descendants of the Arab conquerors of ancient Persia, who repressed my forebears and forced them to flee en masse, have to go. Our culture, one we've kept alive all these centuries. Since the Sixth Century, BCE. AD, for you Christians."

"You can't just send a note to the Arab Iranians and expect them to pick up and leave."

"No. I can't. But I learned some things over the past few years. In the South of France, a small nuclear device was secreted into a Marseille Arab neighborhood, and detonated. The French government's leaders immediately congregated in Paris. An attempt to blow them all up with a similar device went South, as you'd say. In west China, a similar technique was deployed. In that Muslim semi-autonomous state."

"So I heard." Crayle didn't elaborate that his Blackstone Strategy had prescribed those very events. The result, both France and China had evolved into Illuminé dominions.

"I have a dilemma. My plan can't use Muslims as scapegoats. How can I get the leadership of Iran to congregate so I can blow them up?"

"Can you get the job done without explosives?"

The Parsi laughed. "My first thought was to steal Mecca's Black Cube, the Kaaba. Then, transport it secretly, of course, to Tehran, and make it look like the leaders were behind the theft. The Muslims of the world would descend upon them."

Crayle processed his host's scheme. "Have you considered seeing a psychiatrist? That idea pushes the outer boundaries of insanity."

The Parsi laughed again, and topped off the whiskey. "How then would you strategize it, Mr. Crayle?"

"How about you get the Iranian people to overthrow the government? The set up would be to make you Parsis god-like so they would qualify as the ruling class of the new Persia. A return to the glory and grandeur of the past that was lost in modern Iran. As Zoroastrians, you could easily promise to no longer engage in, or foster, religious violence in the Middle East, or the rest of the world."

His host took a long pull of whiskey, then refilled the glass. "My, my. That would be credible, and we could restore the honor of Persia in the process."

"You'd need your own intelligence operation up front. Spies to foment an insurgency."

An epiphany pierced the growing stupor of the Parsi. "We could smuggle operatives in through southeastern Iran."

"How so?"

"There exists traffic along the northern shores of the Arabian Sea." He pointed out a large window. "West from India, along the Pakistan coast, to the port at Bandar Beheshti."

"Isn't the current traffic monitored? Boats and their cargos inspected? That could be a problem."

His host gave a third laugh. "Corruption reigns, Mr. Crayle. The fishing boats are of no interest to the authorities. The rest, the contraband boats bringing drugs, sex slaves, and so forth to Iran from Pakistan, are a constant source of some very serious bribes. Wealth-enhanced officials and guards make docile officials and guards."

"It seems you have a plan, then."

"With your help, I do. I am most grateful." He lifted his glass. "To Persia!"

They toasted.

As Crayle sat back, his furtive mind went right to work on the details. Which, he knew, was where the Devil resided.

CHAPTER 18

The two women returned to the villa from the Mumbai Hard Rock Café.

Hekka pulled up before the two men. Looping one handle of her Hard Rock logo'd bag, she reached in and withdrew a T-shirt. She spread it across her torso with, "Well?"

Chuckles from the men.

Her new friend made the obvious observation.

"Put men together with booze, and they rewrite the history of the women who came before their current one-and-onlys."

Hekka started to share a laugh with her new friend, Leonor, but the transformation on her husband's face stopped her.

"Pattie!"

The Parsi, still laughing at his wife's humor, turned to Crayle.

"Pattie?"

"Never mind her. I have things of import to tell you. Things that must not leave this room." Crayle nodded at Modi's wife.

"Leonor is with me, now and forever. She will hold an important and necessary position. She can and must listen. She's very discreet."

Crayle nodded his agreement. Both women would stay and hear.

"Please listen carefully, Rusty. Pour yourself a few more fingers of *Officer's Choice Black*. Relax. Here goes."

Modi poured as his guest, now in charge, suggested. He did want to hear what this American mastermind would say.

"You clearly are aware of my systems expertise. That I could help you identify optional approaches to solving your problem. Not to trivialize it in just a few words, but you want Persia back. And all that entails, except the extensive land holdings part in ancient times that would extend far beyond Iran's current borders.

"You wish to restore Persian culture, and its attitude that those who don't win, lose. America and the so-called West have had nothing but problem after problem with the Islamic State of Iran—their characterization, not ours. Right away, I see common ground. If our president agrees with me, you will not hear that on TV. Or see it in social media. It would need to be highly classified at my end, and yours."

"Then, how do we communicate?"

"We'd get you a special phone. It would only work with mine. Off the books entirely. If, or should I say when, you succeed, President Stones will work out a relationship with you and your new Persia that will bring prosperity like you've never before experienced."

Modi considered the heady soliloquy he'd just heard. And took a serious gulp of whiskey.

"If your president is still there. In the White House."

"We'll need to work fast. Expedite. We'll stay in touch. But you'll have to have your reigning structure, people, constitution—the whole works—ready. We're close to the end of the year now. By this time next year, I want to see this done. And, from what I know, it'll have to be. Got it?"

"In your own words, got it."

They shook hands … on the deal … and to say goodbye.

Leonor shuttled them back to the Constellation.

CHAPTER 19

Micmac sat at the work table in his cabin when his Science and Technology issue Smartphone rang. Crayle. Their verbal meanderings were safe since, over time, the former SEAL had modified his space into a makeshift Sound and Technology Isolated Facility. No signals came in or out of the STIF without Micmac enabling them. They were enabled now.

Crayle spoke first. "You've created a number of wonderful gadgets for the CIA's Second Directorate. Cutting edge snowflakes, and so forth. We need to step this up on the next project."

"You have something in mind, don't you?" The Crayle team member stepped to and from the kitchen sink, sporting a pair of orange-slice-garnished pints of Blue Moon. He placed them on the table, then retook his seat.

"We've had our first manufactured virus attack," Crayle said. "We survived. We're prepared for subsequent attacks due to President Stones' quick and pervasive actions."

"If I follow, we can't lose focus on the other two categories of NBC warfare. We dealt well with the biological weapon. But we can't ignore the possibilities our adversaries might implement with chemical and nuclear weapons."

Crayle took a long hard listen to Micmac, taking a determined sip of the ice cold beer. "After just these few years, you read me like a book."

He listened as Micmac squeezed the orange slice and took a more serious pull. "Ahhh. And next, you will define for me the problem, my dear Mag, and what the solution is required to affect."

"You understand well the Systems Approach to complex problem solving that I mastered. We proceed."

Micmac sat back and nursed the delicious beer. As much as he wanted to quaff it in one take, those sorts of sailor behaviors were far in the rear view mirror.

"We'll focus on the nuclear. The proliferation has already occurred. Stemming further devastation is necessary, but doesn't eliminate the risk."

"I feel some history coming on."

"Yes. Back in the early 1970s, there was an estimate. In brief, the United States and Soviet Union possessed sufficient nuclear weaponry to scald the planet to lifelessness. Forty times over."

"That would make humanity and all other life forms extinct, wouldn't it?"

"And likely for eternity. With the resurgence of the global Communist ideal, the Russian and American weaponry is being returned to operational status."

"But the Communist elite must cripple us before the president can have our own nuke stuff back to full readiness in that regard."

"Just so," Crayle agreed.

"We need an updated Mutually Assured Destruction?"

"Actually, Prevented Destruction. I call it MPD. Our scientists worked in the 70's under the assumption the Soviets would launch their nuclear-tipped missiles from land or sea, and we would be able to respond in kind before their weapons made landfall."

"And you propose?"

"A new capability. As soon as an enemy fires up the delivery system, we detonate their nuke. Remotely."

"Whoa! Now there's a hack!"

Crayle smiled. "Yes. A hack. There's nothing to demotivate our adversaries like a nuclear event on their own soil if they should make the ultimate, unacceptable decision."

"What about testing? We clear that with known-nuke nations before we do that?"

"The perfect time for the first incarnation of my new strategy."

"Wow. I'm seeing an app here."

"Classified TS for now. We'll bring in the president and Science and Technology when we have something." He paused. "Your mission, Mr. MacKay ..."

"I'll get right on it ... uh ... Mr. Phelps."

"Before I go, just one thing more. I've heard from Ling. She needs more assistance. I'm kind of tied up here, so I'd appreciate it if you gave her a call."

Crayle hung up.

Micmac had been around the block. He finished the first beer, then went after the second with a vengeance. He feared that something serious was about to take place. In Hong Kong. And, truth be told, he wanted to see her again.

CHAPTER 20

It was the President of the United States, calling his favorite spy, Magus Crayle. His spy knew the ring tone. He also knew from substantial experience how his own priorities could change in a heart beat. He touched ***RECEIVE***, and listened.

"Hi, Mag. I had a moment and did a little reminiscing. A few questions popped up that just won't go away. Got a moment?"

"For the leader of the Free World, I do."

"I know it seems like long ago, but if my presidential memory serves me, it was less than a year. Anyway, I ask you to take out the source of the Chinese mini-nukes, you go to see your Empress Ling friend, and shortly thereafter, the entire manufacturing facility deep underground blows up."

"I had a little help, Sir. Ling and Micmac deserve major credit."

"I'm sure they do. Forget that 'sir' crap." He gave it a second. "How the hell did you take out the final remnants of her opposition—the ones setting up to nuke Hong Kong Palace—with her and everyone else in it—in order to regain power?"

"Good fortune. The former China leaders who survived the Beijing nuke—the remnants of the old Communist standing committee—went to the bomb makers to get one for the palace. We had it on surveillance video."

"You were far away. How'd you detonate the reactor?"

"A minor hack into their system, and we goosed the enrichment process … to beyond unstable. *Poof!*"

"*Poof?* Dud firecrackers go poof. You took out the whole vineyard topside, and the surrounds. I'd give you another medal if I didn't have to deny our part in this."

"I believe one Medal of Freedom is sufficient. Sir."

"And stop that 'sir' shit. Anyone who braves a full-scale blizzard blowing across the Bering Sea in order to drag me over an ice bridge between the two Diomede Islands …"

"You left out the pursuit by a segment of the Russian Federation Army. And the vicious dogs."

"So I did. So I did. But I didn't call you for any of that. It's about the DCI job. You promised, I know, but losing the world's best operative from the field in the current volatile circumstance just might outweigh potentially the best DCI ever. I'm conflicted."

Crayle smiled. "I can't quite feel your pain from way over here."

"I've been thinking of taking the self-styled demi-gods at intel, and shoving sharpened poles up their asses. Then displaying them across the White House lawn."

"Like Vlad the Impaler? In Transylvania?"

"Speaking of Vlad, today's intel briefing gave his body up as being in transit from Iran back to Russia. Cause of death?"

"Overdose of Novichok."

Stones sat there stunned. "How … how'd you know?"

"Ear to the ground and such."

"I'm taking some more time on the DCI decision. Sommers is keeping the lid on stuff, at what you two call The Company. Where are you and Hekka, anyway?"

"India. She needs to complete her research here. Perhaps another week or two."

Stones let out a long breath. "So I'm giving you a pass for now. In return, I need a little favor."

"Well, Hekka's locked in research and, good news, has made a new friend to help her right here in Mumbai. I have a couple of days free. So, what's up?"

"I need you to grab the Falcon 8X, and hop on over to Paris. The new French king needs a dose of your advice."

"Hop? From India to France? What the hell could Jean-Marc want?"

CHAPTER 21

It may not have been a cold day in Hell, but it certainly was a cold day in Paris. The recently crowned new king found himself, once again, in a back and forth with his main squeeze, the Queen of Sweden. *Repartee* is a French word. And Jean-Marc, the new King of France, was very French.

"We should have children," said the queen.

"I don't believe we're married."

"Last night indicated to me that marriage is not an impediment."

"Nor all those nights before. I think the French people struggle with the idea of a foreigner as their queen."

"Oh! Foreigner am I? Your father, Sylvain, as he became king for a day, chose that Pattie Norbrunn tart as his queen. She was actually Dutch."

"Ah, but like you, she was royalty."

"What? The daughter of a mere prince?"

"Something happens when you add 'of Monaco' to the prince thing."

"Let's marry on Christmas Day. Right here in Versailles."

"Or in the recently reconstructed Notre Dame Cathedral. By the pope."

"You may have something. Why a mere priest or cardinal when you can get a pope. Unfortunately, there is a fly."

"In the ointment?"

"You're such a stud with those Americanisms."

"About that fly …"

"Oh. Yes. I'm, as you know, biblically and otherwise, Swedish. We are Lutheran, and keep our distance from the Roman Catholic guilt. Adherents, as Martin Luther so eloquently put it, *were* actually guilty."

"I'll make a deal. I shall absorb all of the guilt for both of us. There."

"Done, then. When do we marry, and where?"

A bell chimed, followed by the entrance of a Nineteenth-Century-garbed man. "Your guest has arrived."

"Show him in, Richelieu. And bring us an '82 Bordeaux. Mouton-Rothschild. And three glasses."

"*Oui, monseigneur.*" He left.

Two minutes later, the weary traveler stepped into the room.

"Magus Crayle," Jean-Marc said as he stood to receive his guest.

"Jean-Marc. First, my condolences regarding your father's death."

"I'm a bit surprised. He tried to kill you and your team many times."

"Well, he achieved his lifelong dream of avenging his beheaded, aristocratic ancestors by becoming King Louis XIX. Although death at his wife's hand on his inauguration day was rather dramatic, I believe he rests in peace."

"Well, thank you, monsieur."

"As you are aware, America has an ambassador to France. Why did you specify my presence via President Stones?"

"An ambassador won't do. Your Blackstone Strategy overthrew the French government, which allowed us to re-establish this monarchy. We've seen how the geopolitical power of those small nuclear devices—used at just the right time and in just the right place—can affect drastic change. While it was once an advantage, I worry that one or more of these bombs could make a return to France. It's necessary to be aware of my country's democratic underbelly. We've spent far too much time and effort to get here. How do we stop them?"

"The world is down to just a few mini-nuclear devices left. As you've probably heard, the bomb-making operation in China went up in smoke. Everything's gone, including the scientists."

"You're sure of this?"

"My team and I saw to it personally."

"May I ask how?"

"Assisted by the new Chinese Empress, we hacked into their system, and heated things up a bit. The volatility went beyond red-line, and *poof!*"

"*Poof?* A bunch of nuclear warheads don't go poof."

"You're right. It was quite dramatic. Bottom line, there are only six left."

"Six!"

"Not to worry. They're far from France and even from Europe in general. In a new place. Not formally part of the Illuminé continents."

Jean-Marc carefully considered Crayle's comment. "We've done Europe, East Asia, Australia … I've got it! It must be Africa! The bombs are in Africa. You might help us still. Our beloved France has interests there."

"I'll do what I can." He took a long pull from his wine glass. He wasn't about to give up the Parsi and the South Asian subcontinent. But then, Rusty would need only three. Could the others be headed for Africa? Or already be there? Perhaps another long talk with Kimbel Stones. "It appears your Illuminé is about done, Jean-Marc."

The Swedish Queen displayed a serious frown. "Wait a minute. That's right. You are a member of that secret society. The enlightened. The Illuminé!"

"I've achieved my goal. No further action required. And with the society's leader, the Elder, dead, I do think that's all behind me … us."

"That's not what I meant." She beamed. "That entire society was founded for highly intelligent atheists. Catholicism won't be a problem. Let's get married tomorrow!"

"Let's see," Crayle intervened. "France gets itself a new queen by a justice of the peace. I don't believe that's been done."

The pair looked at him like he had at least two heads.

She tugged Jean-Marc toward the bedroom.

"Please, Mr. Crayle. Follow us into the bed chamber. We can continue our conversation there. Unless you'd be embarrassed."

"I'm sure I can glean some new and precious intel sitting next to your bed."

Jean-Marc laughed as he passed through the ornate double doors. "If you can make something out of Oh! Oh! Oh!"

CHAPTER 22

It was trending cool in Paris this late in the year. But the rebuild of Versailles, since Pattie's mini-nuke had leveled it, brought it up to extremely heightened climate control capabilities in its interior. A perfect 72 degrees Fahrenheit. Or 22 and change Celsius.

The new dawning fired a round of sunlight through the Louis XIV drapes. Crayle had spun on his heel and left the royal love birds to their successor-creating activities the night before. A sumptuous and comfortable couch had sufficed for a pleasant night's sleep. He'd bring Hekka here some day, as guests of the royals, of course.

He liked the notion of friends in high places, though most of his arch enemies had been in high places. Make that, deadly enemies.

The gleeful couple emerged from the bedroom. "Join us for breakfast, Mr. Crayle. Croissants blessed by a cardinal."

"Hmmm. I had a brand new baseball cap blessed by a cardinal once."

"How so?"

"The cardinal flew over after stuffing himself with something that upset his stomach. In Saint Louis."

"If I do well by my people, perhaps I will become a Saint Louis."

"This one's in Missouri."

Puzzled looks.

"Never mind. I'll keep in touch with updates on the nukes. As I said, you shouldn't have to worry. You, Jean-Marc, make your relationship to the lady formal, and you, my dear queen, make some future princes and princesses to give this new royal family substance."

The three smiles were interrupted by a special ring on Crayle's Smartphone. "Is there a place I can take this? Secure?"

Jean-Marc laughed. "This is a royal palace. But here, step into this closet."

He opened a door. "Press the DOWN arrow. The room goes deep and turns into a STIF, I believe you call it. Your signal will be five bars. UP arrow brings you back."

CHAPTER 23

Saint Petersburg, Russia turned out to be somewhat colder than Paris this late in the year. The light snow on the ground provided punctuation to that geographic reality.

Crayle walked the long hall of the Catherine Palace with its artist-painted ceiling, inlaid floor, many arched windows, and adorned on sides and ends with more gold adornments than paint. With five bulky Russians trailing. Four bodyguards, and Raspi.

"She's in here." Raspi pointed to a doorway.

"Should I go in? You said she's not feeling—"

"Please. Enter."

Crayle did. He found the royal bedroom sumptuous, and then some. And there before him lay the Czarina, first female modern day head of the vast Russian land, and the only one since Catherine the Great died in 1795, with covers pulled up to hide at least half of her ample breasts.

"Welcome to Anastasia's palace, Mr. Crayle."

"It bears a striking resemblance to that of Catherine the Great."

"Out with the old, as you say, in with the new. Cat and I do share a few proclivities, however."

"I've come a long way. That you successfully appealed your needs to President Stones scores major points."

"As you have no doubt guessed, we can speak freely here. The room has been swept for bugs by Raspi himself." She nodded toward the man half-hidden along a shadowed wall.

"*Privyet, tovarishch*," the man croaked.

"And greetings again to you, comrade," Crayle returned. He noted the residual semblance of Communistic reference, but quickly refocused on the czarina and awaited the obvious.

"Please, Raspi. Privacy?"

Raspi gave a slight bow of the head, and backed thru a hidden wall panel.

Crayle felt an apology seemed appropriate. "Your chief advisor said you weren't feeling well. I …"

"I'm not feeling well … yet," she said, peeling back the sheets to reveal her naked body.

"Uh. You may have, in Russia, a different perception of marital status than in the States."

"I wouldn't ask you to do anything you wouldn't do with your wife. Come, make yourself at home."

Noticing there weren't any chairs, he took a seat on the centuries-old bed. Just beyond the Czarina's reach.

"Don't worry about the age of the bed. It can take a pounding."

He relaxed just a bit. "I'll take your word on that."

"My FSB is working on a drug having the same effect as hypnosis. A mere keyworded suggestion, and I could have my way with you."

"Ah, yes. *Federalnaya Sluzhba Bezopasnosti*. Well, until your domestic spy agency perfects this new wonder drug …"

"*Xorosho*. Okay." Anastasia climbed from the bed and donned a light blue and gold nightgown more reminiscent of a gentleman's club garment than a cover up. She stepped close enough to place her right hand on his chest. Then, backed away. "But first, I have a goal and need your expertise."

She stepped out onto her balcony, leaning over the rail.

It was exceptionally cold this late in the year in Saint Petersburg. She didn't seem to mind.

"Turning your back on an American spy? Pretty risky."

"At this point, I usually expect something from behind."

"Yes. Well. About Iran, and your relationship there."

She straightened, and turned to face the very handsome, charismatic man who leaned against the door frame.

The quite sexual Czarina couldn't let the notion pass.

"The best I can hope is that it's business before pleasure with you."

"Just business." Crayle recalled the Joe Friday line from an ancient TV cop series. *Just the facts, Ma'am.*

"If something—natural, of course—should happen to your beautiful spy wife ..."

"Iran?"

She huffed. "Let's go inside. Without that special inner warmth I anticipated, it's too cold out here."

A few seconds later, they were seated before an Eighteenth Century fireplace.

The Czarina fingered a remote. A silent vacuum sucked up an existing pile of ashes. The back canted away from them, a new set of dry logs appeared, and the back returned to its upright posture. A moment later, a flame set the wood afire.

"Upgrades," she informed. She placed the remote on a Czar Nicholas table. "Iran has been locked onto Russian influence for many years. Vladimir was prepared to supply that country with nuclear bomb materials. Then, supervise the building of the weapons. One thing you should understand. The power of the Grand Ayatollah is not merely grand, it's absolute. To gain control, Vlad merely needed to co-opt the top cleric. And he did."

"So he either gave him a bunch of Russian Rubles—worth their weight in dog crap—or had something big on him. Worthy of extortion."

"The latter. Our external spy agency, the SVR, discovered his association with the Illuminé secret society."

"I wonder how they accomplished that."

"Nicely done, Magus."

"First names at a later date." He immediately regretted portending a personal relationship.

For her part, she pressed her palms together and produced a wicked smirk.

Crayle moved quickly. "The elite religious community at the top of the heap in Iran would take unkindly to their exalted leader being outed as an atheist, like all members of the enlightened Illuminé."

"In short, the good people of Iran would stage a huge bonfire in Tehran, utilizing the aforementioned clerics as the primary fuel."

Crayle nodded agreement. "But the Ayatollah went with the Chinese mini-nuke. Vlad must've felt his grip on Iran slipping. Or had slipped."

"He fumbled Iran right into Chin Yao-wu's hands. China and Russia have long been adversaries. Only Communism bound them together."

"And the Gorbachev political chess miracle, *Perestroika*, set that aside, at least for public consumption."

She could see they were on the same page. "Yes. The so-called Chicoms could no longer be friends with a nation that had willfully changed the bonds of the most extreme leftist ideology for Life, Liberty, and the Pursuit of Happiness."

"But it was all fake. The closet Communists here still ran the country, and poured huge resources into pulling down America. From within."

The Czarina sighed. "They're still at work. Although your president is tearing at the framework. I just might have a list of names of the seditionists here somewhere."

She gave him a sly look.

Crayle realized he could've written her next line in one of his novels.

"You know, a spy must make sacrifices to obtain valuable intelligence, perhaps without bounds, for the sake of his country."

"Something tells me you have some really light weight sacrifices in mind."

He was interrupted at that point by a code-syncopated vibration in his pants. He extracted the errant Smartphone.

"Can I take this call somewhere safe?"

She frowned. Then, held her hand, palm to cheek with thumb and pinky extended. "Let's see. Call me at …"

The Czarina glanced over at him. "… what time is it?"

"It's my wife. She's wondering where I am."

CHAPTER 24

Magus Crayle continued on with Czarina Anastasia Romanov at her palace in St. Petersburg, Russia. He needed to figure out this most recent Jack Sommers episode, resolve whatever problems were at issue, then get back to Hekka. ASAP.

"As you know, Vladimir succeeded in establishing himself as czar, and me as his mate. I have the Romanov bloodline, he had the president and leader of Russia provenance."

"Things went a bit South in Iran, didn't they?"

"Yes. Our carryover SVR spy agency had permanent residence in Tehran. I received their account of Vlad's demise from the SVR head personally."

"I'm curious. Where did you bury him?"

"Your arrival today is a coincidence. His casket is due here any time now."

"You didn't ask President Stones to have me here to pay my respects. What is it you want? Nuke Tehran? Indirectly?"

"You have the nuke portion correct. But, no, my problem is local."

"St. Petersburg?"

"No, Mr. Crayle. Moscow."

"You want to blow up the capitol of Russia?"

"Long story short. The extreme ideology known as Communism has not been on the ropes, as you might say, but rather has been in hiatus for a few decades. While China has borne the flag, and the attention of the capitalist West, Russia has secretly re-birthed the hammer and sickle as a political virus already spreading here, and in the West."

"If they succeed, your reign will be short-lived."

"With the emphasis on *lived.* They will ceremoniously execute me, as they did my ancestors in 1918. But only after America and its all-powerful economic system has been brought to its knees."

Crayle recalled his recent trip to Hong Kong.

"As by a biological weapon? Say, a pandemic virus?"

"Vladimir met with the Chinese leader to set up, at the highest level, such an attack. Something tells me that the application of a bio-weapon against your country is not new to you. What do you know, Mr. Crayle?"

"I know that the Chinese secretly developed a treatment and a vaccine. To precede deployment of such a weapon. You send human disease vectors to the U.S., hit population-dense centers, inflict medical workers, and ***boom***, the quarantine of a nation. Prolonged, the American economic miracle starts to unwind. As links in the chain dissolve—become insolvent—the whole thing crashes and burns."

"The democracy is blamed, and the forerunner of a Communist America, masquerading as merely Socialist, is poised to 'save' the people. Venezuela was the test case. Vlad shared all of his grand schemes with me."

"Let me guess. It gets so bad, the new government suspends constitutional requisites such as human rights."

"He told me so. Freedom of movement goes. Free speech goes. Right to trial. Right to representation. Right to assemble and protest."

"And, finally, the right to choose those who govern."

"Exactly. The government that worked for the people becomes the people who work for the government."

"We've seen this before. The Soviet Union. Seventy years of repression."

"Will you help me stop them?"

"Are you familiar with my Blackstone Strategy?"

"You mean, get them all in one place … and blow them up?"

"That's the one."

CHAPTER 25

The President of the United States had plenty of work piled up in the Oval Office. Europe, the incessant Middle East, East Asia, et cetera, et cetera. Stepping out for a couple of hours just allowed the pile to get deeper. But he needed to speak with Jack Sommers. In person.

He pressed a button under his famous desk to provide an indication to those outside. He was not to be disturbed. It was well known that his Secret Service protectors didn't like being shut out. For any period of time. For any reason. Kimbel Stones then proceeded via a secret passageway. The one-person elevator descended both silent and quick.

Deep in the bowels beneath the White House, he strapped himself into the warp speed rail transport pod. With bleeding edge technology obtained from Germany, the vehicle sped him Southwest at nearly 300 miles per hour, toward Manassas, Virginia. To the lair of the off-books Strategic Solutions Office three hundred feet below the Manassas National Battlefield Park.

Every time he tried to utilize the transit time to think, the rocky tunnel surrounds flying by at close to 300 miles per hour proved a distraction. What was this thing about the number 300, he wondered.

He soon arrived and made his way to the Sound and Technology Isolated Facility, or STIF.

"Sitrep, Jack. I sent Mag to Paris, dark on the communications side, due to the sensitivity of the operation. What does your resource at Versailles say about the meeting he had with the new king?"

Jack related what his resource, the Queen of Sweden, had related just two hours after Crayle departed Versailles.

"So now we're protecting a monarchy in France."

"Yes, Sir. It was a constant battle with the previous, elected administration. Jean-Marc wants prosperity for his people. No eating of cake for the masses. Champagne and snails."

"Escargot, Jack"

"Given their military history, the snails are the only things slow enough to not get away."

"Now that's harsh."

Apropos of the subject matter, Jack answered with a French shrug.

The president checked his watch. "How about Russia? Be brief."

"My asset in Saint Petersburg says all went well."

"Did your resource bed our asset as she reportedly does everyone else?"

"One, our asset, Mag Crayle, wouldn't go there. Even if you, as president, ordered him to. Two. The Czarina isn't our resource."

"So who is?"

"NTK, Mr. President."

Stones wedged his eyebrows together. Then, "Need To Know? Very funny, Jack. I define security, and am personally cleared for everything."

Jack responded with a bleak smile.

"Mr. Sommers. May I remind you …" Stones broke into a smirk that descended into a belly laugh.

Jack at first thought that the man opposite had lost that final screw. The one that'd been loose for a while now. But, no. The President of America and leader of the free world needed an out of control *let go* more frequently now in the face of nuclear weaponry being unleashed as implements of strategic manifestation.

"Okay," the president said as he regained composure and rose. "That covers my two requests. I wonder where he's off to next. Mumbai? To hook back up with Hekka? And explain to her his absence for several days?" He glanced over at Jack.

"Best you don't know, Mr. President."

"Wait. Mag is blacked out comms wise. How ..."

"IJK. I Just Know."

"I'll have them rendition your lifeless body ..."

Jack gulped.

"Hong Kong."

The president snatched a breath.

"Holy hell!"

CHAPTER 26

Micmac followed Ling's instructions explicitly. He'd agreed to be transported, as an operative, to the locale of the virus lab. Then, he would perform a reconnaissance to determine if the man in question, Ling's biological father, was in residence. Utilizing his SEAL skills, he would then determine securable routes of ingress and egress so that Ling and any entourage she chose to bring along would be as safe as one could be entering a Category 4 virus laboratory.

Ling had been explicit in her desires. She just wanted to see and speak with the father she never knew. Why had he abandoned her? And why had her mother done the same? And was she still alive—her name had not been disclosed in the orphanage documents.

It wasn't until the long ride North beneath Victoria Harbour that concerns began to invade his mind. Ling had made clear that the palace environment was likely to have far more spies than cockroaches.

His ride drove along the New Territories to a paper mill. Micmac reasoned in jest that the location made sense. Older researchers likely clung to writing their notes and research documents in pen and ink—brush and ink in this case—rather than on computers. What better location for a proliferate scientist than proximate to a paper mill?

He checked the driver again.

The woman pointed to a paper with Chinese Sinograms, bobbed her head up and down, recognized the blank look on her passenger's face, then waved her hand toward the office door on the building's side.

Micmac thanked her, returned her head bow, and stepped out of the limo. He quickly crossed the forty paces to the door, and knocked. Nothing. He tested the knob, pushed the door open, and stepped inside.

• • •

Things had gone South in short order. Nicely done, he thought. He'd transitioned from an excessively trained SEAL and espionage operative to a man wishing cobwebs out of his head, as well as release from the restraints confining him to a gurney.

He checked out his captor. Page Boy cut jet black hair with burgundy-tinged surface. A coke bottle figure which bulged in all the right places.

Cheekbones, a perfect nose, dark processed eye brows. By all accounts, a beautiful woman.

"What is your purpose, Mr. MacKay?"

Her tone was anything but casual.

"My mission is highly classified. If you promise not to tell, here goes. I've been directed to make love to all the beautiful women in the country."

She considered the prospects. "All of them?"

"Including yourself. I am to begin as soon as possible."

She liked the humor, but never let it interfere with her work. She extracted a metal device from her satchel. "Some get sexually aroused by the sights and sounds of torture. Perhaps I am so inclined." She stepped toward him and, with her free hand, loosened his belt.

This wasn't going well, Micmac concluded. He needed a new tack. He needed it now.

CHAPTER 27

Crayle arrived in Hong Kong in the morning. The fog had yet to lift, and the airport was closed. Pilot Marli simply called in a Mayday, made her way through the gray soup, and affected a light-as-air touch down as if the whole event reflected standard operating procedure. The less than impressed authorities restrained themselves in this instance. The business jet transported a close friend of Empress Ling, they'd been informed. Their smiles and abbreviated bowing, as the plane's contents filed by, did appear a little strained.

The palace guest limousine transited from the Hong Kong airport to Kowloon with its special guest, American spy Magus Crayle. As it made its way toward the Victoria Harbour Tunnel, he asked the driver to stop. As in, "*Stop!*"

Fearing an impending disaster of which she was woefully unaware, she ran the vehicle to the road's side, and halted it with everything but a screech.

Her passenger stepped out onto the sidewalk in a surprising, calm fashion.

Some memories are nowhere to be found when you want them, and some linger on the mind when you want them gone.

And it'd all started out with Frenchman, Sylvain Lalumière. Lalumière and his water diamonds.

The Star Ferry Station to his right reminded him of his own many passings to and fro, facilitated by the metro transit Octopus proximity card—a must in this town. Then, he gazed behind at the hyper-upscale Peninsula Hotel, ferrying its patrons about town in their ubiquitous green Rolls Royces.

Finally, he glanced up at the 118 story, 1600 foot tall International Commerce Building. The ICC. It was a time long ago, he recalled, but not that long. He and his crew resided at the Victoria Harbour Grand, on the Hong Kong Island side, and about two miles from Central. The better memory had them all sitting in the 42nd floor, atrium-like Le 188° Restaurant and Lounge. At about 8 p.m., much to their surprise, a light show began over the harbor. Green lasers seemingly from everywhere. In awe, they viewed The Symphony of Lights, an every evening occurrence, their waitress informed them.

Unfortunately, their stay devolved into a number of gun battles. Just a two minute walk up Oil Street sat the Fortress Hill subway station. Lenny, long time team member and royal pain in the ass, had performed well there. Then, other locations in Hong Kong. Across the harbor. Up Victoria Peak. So long ago, it seemed, but only a couple of years.

With the remnants of the former China government attempting to destroy their successor and arch-nemesis, Chin Yao-wu.

But, back to the brighter side. Accompanying the light show, the side of the highest building in Hong Kong, right behind him, had come alive with words and pictures, moving from the ground level, up the side, and disappearing at the top. Of supreme note, the unexpected and enigmatic "***WOOF!***"

He still didn't know what that was all about.

Perhaps he'd have time after he provided Micmac with any assistance he might render. Perhaps he'd revisit the splendid hotel. At just the right time.

Then, he thought. No. He'd view the laser show from the palace, say goodbye to Ling, then back to Mumbai. To Hekka.

• • •

The rest of the drive completed as they processed through the Imperial Palace gates atop Victoria Peak. Crayle was surprised to find Ling plus entourage waiting for him on the steps outside the reception hall's giant front doors. As soon as it halted, she hopped into the limo.

"Oh, it's wonderful to see you!" She pecked his cheek.

"Same. But, where's Micmac?"

"I don't know, Magus!" she said with excitement in her voice. Too much.

"Did he meet someone since he's been here? Someone he might have gotten to know."

Ling stopped a second, then decided not to relate how close he'd come to getting to really know her. She recounted her discovery of her birth father, and how Micmac had set off to the man's workplace, the virology lab, to check him out.

"Then I suggest I follow the trail, and see if I can locate him. And chastise him. And return him here so he can share what he discovered."

"I hoped you would say that." She gave a flurry of instructions to the driver, in Chinese, another peck on the cheek to her guest, then stepped out.

The driver didn't waste time. She was moving as soon as Ling had stepped back far enough. Out through the ornate palace gates, and heading down Victoria Peak.

• • •

Crayle's driver had her instructions. She followed the same route to the virus lab as had Micmac. Why the man hadn't checked in remained a mystery. Since the *Mysteries R Us* motif persisted throughout the life of this particular spy team, the situation didn't cause any trepidation.

He was met at the door by a woman with burgundy-tinged black hair wearing a white lab coat, and carrying a clipboard. With no further ado, she showed him into a laboratory that sported all of the usual hardware. Directly ahead, a simple, light yellow desk and its occupant.

The man looked every bit the scientist. He was tall, for a Chinese, 5'10" and looked familiar. Slender, not bulky.

"You stare at me, Mr. Crayle. I remind you of someone, an uncle perhaps."

"Actually, you are the spitting image of Dr. No. From the eponymous Bond movie. Tallish. Slender. Even your elocution is similar."

"It won't surprise you if I say I've heard this before."

"I'm not surprised."

"Allow me to guess that you are not a virologist, like myself, as you've advertised to gain entrance and an audience. In fact, Mr. Crayle, I have access to an extensive data base of adversaries."

"We've never met. Why would you consider me an adversary?"

The man managed a brief smile. A quasi-smile. He fetched a pair of Erlenmeyer flasks from a shelf behind, and a bottle of dark amber liquid. He poured. "There. Three fingers. Shall we toast?"

Crayle, with degrees in mathematics, didn't need them for the simple arithmetic logic presented. Doctor Li had a special data base and drank expensive scotch. A trait shared with operatives spanning the globe. "Illuminé."

"You see, we shall take over the world. A matter of time, that's all."

"You won't be doing it with miniature nuclear weapons. I and my team have seen to that. Since it's clear to me that you know who I am, and my history, why is your top virus research lab here instead of Wuhan?"

"Wuhan was a red herring. With the purposive launch of the corona virus, we needed a scapegoat, just in case. We sacrificed it. All those inside could testify anywhere and to anyone that the virus wasn't of their doing."

"So the virus was created—or selected from nature—here."

"And from that, you can readily discern the rest. Give it a try."

"You know about my expertise with the Systems Methodology. And the Systems Approach that provides for understanding even the most complex of problems."

"I do. Continue. Please."

"Speculation, of course. And off the top of my head. I've not thought this out. Obviously."

"For those who have the gift—the so-called systems thinkers—it would be intuitive."

"Then, here goes. The Communist government of the time shared the same absolutist notion of every other manifestation of that ideology. Global conquest. And domination. It wasn't just a goal, it was a necessity. Karl Marx indicated that capitalism needed to be wiped out. Otherwise, the prosperity it inevitably brought would leave the Socialists and their extreme incarnation, Communists, with no adherents. Placing the two ideologies side-by-side would reveal who would win."

"Juxtaposing them wouldn't be necessary, would it?"

"No. The world had already witnessed East Germany next to West Germany. North Korea next to South Korea. The Soviet Union versus America. Given the choice, the Capitalists always won. And won big."

"So, we had to turn the globe into one giant commune."

"Or languish. We now have the motivation. But how to take down the Capitalists? Direct confrontation would only yield the physical destruction of China. But, a pandemic virus escaping from a lab in Wuhan. There would be no retribution."

"We couldn't just send the virus to all the Capitalist countries, could we? We would have motive, opportunity, and so forth. Everyone would know."

"Of course. You infected people in Wuhan and let it out to the media so you could play the victim. Meanwhile, you also infected operatives, and sent them overseas."

"Excellent deduction, Mr. Crayle."

"But you'd want them not to show symptoms. And at the same time, be infectious."

"It took us decades to uncover precisely the right virus. With the attributes you've discerned."

"But in Wuhan, you couldn't allow the virus to get out of control. You'd need to recover quickly to restart your economy. That means—"

"It means we developed and thoroughly tested a vaccine and an efficacious treatment ahead of time. We slipped the former into our yearly influenza inoculations in October. For all but a few selected from the opposition to our ideology."

"And you must have selected your overseas operatives, or vectors, from those whom you knew could carry the virus, but not require hospitalization."

"You can see that we started long before anything showed up in public. A systems approach, if I may."

"Your operatives hit America, Europe, the Emirates, and Singapore. All bastions of Capitalism."

"Our intended goal of shutting down those economies was achieved. We controlled the news, and expelled Western media at the appropriate moment. All went precisely to plan, Mr. Crayle."

The American spy took a final drink, and pushed the flask forward.

"Oh, you won't be needing any more. I took the opportunity to wipe the mouth of your flask with something I've been working on. Something new. Even more virulent than the corona species. You have perhaps an hour or so. Too bad I can't include you in the trials. We'd have to list your occupation, and Magus Crayle, American spy, might cause a problem." He sat back and gloated. Of the many attempts, no one previously had been able to pull down this spy of all spies. Li now had that honor.

In the next split second, Crayle was over the desk. A smack to the scientist's left median nerve, then to the forward aspect of the left temple, and the man was out cold.

Quick, Crayle rifled his desk.

There!

A damp gauze pad. No doubt the new virus.

Crayle grabbed a pair of plastic gloves from a nearby dispenser, and snatched the gauze.

With malice aforethought, he pried the mad scientist's jaw open, and wiped down the man's tongue.

"Happy trails, Doctor Li."

Next, he pilfered through the man's lab coat until he located a half-filled vial.

"Antidote," he declared out loud. "Placed there in case I reversed the glasses."

He checked the label.

Chinese.

"Oh, hell!"

He quaffed the remaining fluid.

A woozy feeling overcame him.

Then … why hadn't he thought.

He applied the Death Touch recovery methods he'd also learned from Ling. First, pressure to the point known to the accupressurists as Gall Bladder 20. Left of the spine at the base of the skull. Next, a slap to the trapezium muscle at the bottom of the neck.

He'd find out what he'd just imbibed. He peered down at the prostrate man. "Is this really the antidote?"

The scientist didn't respond. Dead.

Ling's biological father.

• • •

Searching the lab's other room, Crayle found no other adversaries. But he did find Micmac. Strapped to a gurney. Still breathing. Out cold.

It appeared he'd just been drugged. No signs or smells of the virus. Keep him alive. Perhaps as a hostage.

Crayle removed the restraining straps, applied the appropriate Death Touch recovery techniques, and toted a drowsy, but waking Micmac to the car. The driver had them away forthwith.

Back to the palace.

Back to Ling.

CHAPTER 28

Hekka finished her research in India of indigenous peoples and their migrations. She'd acquired valuable intel, as her husband would put it, but had yet to relate the earliest peoples of the Western Hemisphere with those of South Asia.

Still, there'd been no word from her husband. At that point, she found a safe place, and placed a call to a very special individual. One who often helped out by making travel arrangements for off-the-books CIA 'contractors' needing special, and secure in the extreme, handling.

She heard the characteristic up front noises, and imagined her conversation being cryptographically transposed, then scrunched as required for real time voice traffic. At the other end, her dialog would be unscrunched and decrypted, both at lightning speed, and without what Micmac labeled artifacts.

Darryl answered in his signature manner. "Hekka! How the hell are you?"

She pictured the world-class grin to go with the greeting.

He continued. "What can I do for you this fine, but chilly, day in Nova Scotia?"

She related to him her dilemma.

"No problem. Magus contacted me earlier, and he's ready to roll. Back your way."

"He didn't call me. Last I checked I—"

"Sorry to interrupt. He's still running dark, comms wise. I was just getting ready to call you for him so you two could link up and—"

"Sorry to interrupt, too. It seems he's using you as a cutout … from the Company."

"Things do sometimes get a little gray in this business. But, yes."

"What do you have?"

"Well, he has the wheels, er, the plane. But lucky you. There's a cruise ship in Mumbai that's ready to go wheels up … uh …"

"Darryl?"

"Ready to sail at 4 p.m. I've taken leave to register you both under the following name." He told her.

Hekka laughed. "That's good. So he's meeting me at the ship. Here in Mumbai."

"Uh, not exactly. You'll be going aboard alone. When you arrive at your first port of call, that's Muscat in Oman, you are to take excursion OM7. Mag will meet you at the tour bus. You two will stop for some high tea and snacks at a palace hotel. Be sure to sit by yourselves."

"How romantic, Darryl. Will he be wearing a disguise?"

"I knew you'd ask. If you look under the table, he'll have exposed a part of him only you would recognize." He broke into serious laugh mode. When he recovered, he said, "Sorry. A little humor."

"Which mirth, I'm convinced, is widely cherished in dark corridors the world over."

"Why, thank you."

• • •

On the ship, Hekka hit the restaurant for lunch. A table for two without the two. At a similar table immediately to her left sat what appeared to be a nice man and woman. He turned and smiled. "Your name?"

She remembered well her pseudonym as supplied by Darryl. "Bond … Mrs. James Bond. And yours?"

"Bourne," he said. "Jason … and Pattie."

CHAPTER 29

The little side trips that took Crayle from Hekka's side in Mumbai to Paris, to Saint Petersburg, and Hong Kong were in the can, in Hollywood parlance. Relieved to a high degree, he transitioned to being a Jack Air passenger, and made use of its fully stocked bar.

With all that'd been laid on the table in the past couple of days, he found he couldn't sleep. On the way from Hong Kong, then to Muscat, Oman to meet up with Hekka, he researched the Arab country and its capitol city.

He decided to bounce his newfound knowledge, and its relevance to his espionage existence, off pilot Marli Sommers. With just one refueling break along the way in Calcutta, India, the discourse would prove invaluable. Later on. When he impressed his wife.

When Marli started to nod halfway through his soliloquy, he put down his notes, and gave her an oral IV of Rockstar—white can—from the Falcon's fridge.

At 500 miles per hour, the entire trip would encompass six hours plus the hour or so in Calcutta. Or so he calculated. If his calculations were on, he'd be able to grab a taxi at Seeb International Airport, and the rest would fall into place.

And it did.

Just as Hekka glanced at her watch for the fifteenth time, she looked up to see her husband bounding across the concrete tour vehicle pad from the cab. With a big smile and open arms, he nearly took her down when they embraced.

Finally, she disengaged. "Our tour guide awaits." She wafted a hand at the awaiting micro-bus. "Magus, this is our guide and driver, Badar. He helped me with the pronunciation."

Crayle shook the young man's hand, and repeated what he'd heard. "Better. Nice to meet you."

"And I," said the guide. "I will inform you as we drive. You are a bit late, so we must hurry in order to make High Tea at the palace hotel."

"Another Palace Hotel? Like in Mumbai?"

"This one is a hotel that was once a real palace."

"Hmm. A little competition between Oman and India?"

"The Indian people come here … to work."

"Okay. And you have what, two million people here?"

"Three million, according to your CIA."

"So, Badar. Do you moonlight with Omani Intelligence, or is it a relative?"

"Neither. The numbers vary. It depends on whom you ask."

"I noticed you got the *whom* right. Most Americans can't do that."

"We receive a thorough education here."

"Then let's go. High Tea awaits."

• • •

Badar drove the fifteen minute distance South from downtown Muscat, mimicking the shoreline as he did. He provided the dialog he'd promised.

"You can see, our capitol city is cuddled against the coast by the Al Hajar mountains. From this road, you can view the extensive and beautiful beach that defines the northern border of the Sea of Oman."

"The form of government here?" Crayle posed the question, knowing the answer from his research, but not stepping on his guide's toes. And prepared to verify that this guide did not just make things up for the tourists.

"A sultanate."

"So, who's in charge?"

"Sultan Qaboos."

"Qaboos?"

"Yes. He has yet to name a successor."

"So, Sultan Qaboos could be last in line."

Hekka elbowed her husband. No explanation was necessary.

"I have not heard that one before." Badar laughed out loud. At his own humor.

Hekka shook her head. "Let me see. Badar-Crayle … at the Comedy Store."

Their guide ended the sequence with, "We have arrived. In the Al Shati area of town. Please appreciate the Al Bustan Palace Hotel. By Ritz-Carlton."

He pulled up to the overly ornate portico, and alighted with his passengers.

Inside, he showed them around.

Badar didn't need to explain much. This was a palace, or had been, worthy of any sultan.

"And this is the Atrium Tea Lounge." He gestured at the opulence of the walls, the floors, and at the large dome's interior, high above. "Please take a seat. High Tea will be served shortly."

"Thank you, Badar," Hekka said. "Where do we find you when we're finished?"

“That won’t be a problem.” He bowed briefly, turned on his heel, and vanished.

• • •

The light repast and tea drinking only lasted thirty minutes. Crayle related his recent meanderings, cloaking the necessary parts due to the lack of security in the Tea Lounge.

“We just hopped over to Paris from Mumbai,” he began. “No big deal. Doing a favor for Kimbel.”

“Just hopped over? To Paris?”

“Yeah. Then, a second request. Over to Saint Petersburg.”

“Florida?”

“No. The other one.”

“So now you’re in Russia.”

“That’s not all.”

“Please, dig the hole deeper.”

“Then … well … Hong Kong. Just doing favors. You know. To make up for delaying my promise to take over the Company. For Kimbel.” Crayle by now appeared a bit nervous.

“Let me see if I have this right. You traveled several days and many miles with Jack’s lovely ex, Marli, at the controls. Then Paris, with that gorgeous Queen of Sweden. Then, on to Saint Petersburg with the voluptuous sexaholic czarina, Anastasia. Then, the Imperial Palace in Hong Kong. With Ling. Someone with whom you share a serious history.” She waited several beats. “So …”

“Boy, that was fun. We’ve known each other so long we can do that sort of trust-filled banter.” He smiled.

Hekka followed with her own, minimalist smile. “You know how it is with us spies. We trust someone … and then we don’t. It’s why I always keep my Bowie sharp.”

They clinked tea cups.

A beautiful day.

• • •

The Crayles finished their last sip of the mint-flavored tea as Badar appeared, almost like an apparition, nearby.

"Not to rush, but there are aspects of the Al Bustan I simply must show you before we rush off. Your ship has an all aboard today at 4 p.m."

He led them out the back way to a sultan-class pool area. Big enough for as many guests as a ruler could want, plus body guards.

Crayle was impressed. "Beautiful pool. Lounge chairs. Numerous palm trees wafting in the sea breeze."

Badar pointed to their right. "And the shoreline and beach right there, a short walk away." Then, he furrowed his brow. "May I ask, do you have little ones?"

Hekka answered. "We have. One. Our daughter."

Badar then pointed out a playground, and a kid-sized, wooden rendition of an old sailing ship. From its deck, an on-cue little girl slid down a water slide into the pool.

"Oh, Magus. We'll have to come back. Kianna would love it here."

"I'm sure she would," Badar opined. "When she's old enough to swim."

That caught the Crayles' attention.

"By the way," he added. "Mr. Sommers sends his regards."

With his clients thoroughly bewildered, Badar led them back through the hotel to the micro-bus. And drove them, in total silence, back to the ship.

CHAPTER 30

Crayle sat out on his stateroom balcony. He pondered whether Hekka had truly forgiven him, as she'd said, for departing for several days without so much as a word during his absence. She wouldn't have expected a sitrep. Those were for ops. But a "Hi. I miss you. I love you." would have been what she wanted to hear. And that he was safe.

Except, he hadn't stepped outside while she showered to let his mind wander. He dialed his Smartphone, put it to his ear, then slipped the hood Hekka had used on him for Phuket over his head with his free hand. Anyone on a balcony nearby would hear nothing but muffled sounds.

"Hi, Mag," came the dulcet tones of Jack Sommers. "I gotta run so I'll make this quick. Stay aboard for the night passage to Dubai. Uh, the United Arab Emirates."

"I know of the Emirates, Jack. I could just fly to Dubai from here in an hour or so."

"No. I need you to sail there while I put together a team, and get them over there."

"A team? I don't need a team to finish off my trip with Hekka. What—"

"Trust me. You'll need them. Look, you'll pass the night cruising northeast from Muscat and through the Strait of Hormuz, and past the point at the end of the Musandam Peninsula. It's a special piece of Omani territory. Just as you enter The Gulf, you'll see three lights off to port. Just above the water's surface, and not far from shore. Then, past the coastal village, Al Khasab, also to port. If you could see to starboard, there'd be more coastal lights. Iran. You won't be going there."

"What use could they possibly have for a tired, old American spy?"

"You'll want to sit out on your port-side balcony the whole transit time … the sights are more than memorable."

"So, you've been here?"

"No comment."

"I thought you were in a hurry."

"Once you arrive at Port Rashid in Dubai, grab a cab to the Al Murooj hotel." Jack spelled it out. "Room reserved for Mr. Jimmy Bond."

"James was taken?"

"Cute. Enjoy the property tomorrow. Great buffets in the restaurant. Get in some pool time. Grab food at The Edge thirty or so feet away. You'll need to shake off Hekka in the afternoon. You'll hook up with your aforementioned team at 4 p.m. nearby." He provided a pub name and directions. "The place has a British flair."

"So, meet … and potatoes?"

"Save the humor for later. You'll need it."

Crayle took notice. He started to extract what this op requiring a team was all about, but Jack got their first.

"The team knows what you look like. Just walk around until someone gives the verbal handshake. It's 'Quick, Watson.' And you say—"

"We haven't a moment to lose."

"Well done. You've got this. Just keep thinking that."

"But—"

"The whole thing should be over by midnight or so. Hekka will hardly know you've been gone."

"But—"

"Oops. Gotta go. Stay safe, Mag."

Jack clicked off.

Just as Crayle lowered the phone, removed the hood, and shoved both items into his pockets, Hekka opened the sliding glass door. She stepped out onto the balcony, wearing nothing but a towel wrapped around her head.

"Did I miss something?"

"Oh, no," Crayle said with bleary, unseeing eyes.

Then, he managed a smile as he stood, and turned toward her.

"Here. Let's see what you look like undressed."

He stepped close, reached up, and removed the towel.

CHAPTER 31

Crayle turned Hekka onto some pool time. He had to run out for a bit. Be right back.

Down to the lobby. Out the front doors. Turn left. Transit the stairs and landings until you reach the bottom. Turn right. Walk until you see the sign. Go in.

Those were his instructions. Easy to follow. Perhaps, too easy, for what lay ahead.

Crayle entered the Double Decker Pub. He immediately noticed that it seemed filled to capacity at about 250 patrons. He kept his eyes open. His meeting with a four man covert team needed to draw no attention.

The tables all had a three-digit number plate on the outside edge. The system associated, in groups, with their assigned wait staff, and also served to allow regulars to be seated at their usual table.

Three men sat at table 007. Crayle expected four. One of them initiated the pre-planned, verbal handshake. He stepped up to the table, and reached a hand to the man on the left. The one replete in a three-piece, Saville Row suit.

"I'm Dexter," he announced, stealing a pen name from one-time newspaper reporter, now President of the United States, Kimbel Stones.

Crayle noted that meals had been ordered. Bangers and mash. Fish and chips, and an eight-inch high hamburger with two sets of patties, tomato, lettuce, secret sauce, top and bottom buns plus two in the middle, and a note attached. ***Eat the Big Boy Burger in thirty minutes, and it's free – conditions apply***.

The man behind it responded, "I'm Matthew."

Then, the less nattily dressed man in the middle. "I'm Mark."

"I'm Luke." More sportily attired as befitting the pub's sports bar atmosphere.

Crayle furrowed his brow. "Where's the other one?"

"In the John."

Mark pounded the table as the three laughed in a very British manner. In a quiet restaurant, they would've been summarily ejected. Not here. Their raucous behavior was barely audible above the ambient din. Crayle decided to enter the verbal fray. Time to loosen up this trio of operatives.

"Your names have an apostolic feel to them."

"Indicating knowledge … in the biblical sense." More guffaws from the Brits.

"So a lesser team would've been Peter, Paul, and …"

"Mary. Yes, the virgin."

Micmac, operative and musician, came to Crayle's mind. "If three wasn't enough, then surely a pair like, say, the Dubai Brothers …"

Before they could react, a voice came from behind. "Hi, Dexter. I'm Jane."

"Wrapping up … Matthew, Mark, Luke, and Jane. Swell."

He turned, but found no reason to describe her.

The house band began a new set with *Long Cool Woman In A Black Dress*. The characterization described her to a T. That she knew his pseudonym indicated someone in the threesome wore a concealed microphone. She'd been listening. The bathroom positioning provided separation in case she'd be called on for covering fire, should the meet go wrong.

Apostle Mark had the op details, which he began to share. The crowd plus the band precluded understanding what Crayle needed to understand. He shared the trick Micmac had provided at Big Bear Valley's Sugarloafer bar and grill, where the former SEAL and his band entertained.

"Just press the flap on your ear, your best ear, closed. Gently. You can hear every word."

They followed his lead, and Mark began again. They were all impressed. They could clearly hear every word. Impressive American tradecraft. The Second Apostle finished briefing the new addition twenty minutes later with a teaser. "Expect a big surprise."

Matthew checked his watch. Then, "We need to boogie, as you Yanks say."

The four stood as a unit, Crayle followed suit.

They led him to a big black GMC Denali SUV.

"Great cover," Crayle remarked.

Luke drove them around Dubai at normal speeds. He pointed out the sights as they processed past numbers of buildings, no two alike. He turned onto Highway 11.

"IBM, Microsoft, Oracle, Ferrari, Maserati, Bugatti, Lamborghini, Porsche."

Then, some less likely names.

"American Hospital – Dubai. Cleveland Clinic. British Dental Clinic."

Crayle frowned at the last one. "You four Brits going to check in there?"

"Ooh, no way," they all responded.

Two hours later they entered the Emirati capitol, Abu Dhabi.

Luke, the self-appointed travel guide, didn't disappoint.

"Ferrari World. Formula 1 race course. The Emirati version of the Louvre. President's Palace. Heritage Museum over that way. Etihad Tower. And ADNOC. The Abu Dhabi National Oil Company. That one matters. Matthew'll fill you in during the boat ride."

Crayle didn't know what to make of his Surprises R Us tactical team. What could possibly be next?

CHAPTER 32

The stereotypical black ops team SUV stopped at Abu Dhabi's Yas Marina. Ever wary, but trying not to look that way, they made their way onto what Crayle would later term the well-endowed Dhow. The ancient appearing wooden boat sported concealed, silenced cannons and machine guns, as well as rockets, ammo, lasers, and a couple of cruise missiles just in case. The craft affected its propulsion via a pair of turbo jets, which lifted it onto purpose-customized hydrofoil struts.

"We'll be making way toward Doha, the capitol city of Qatar. At least, that's what the documentation says." Matthew gave a wink saying in effect, "We're not going there. Instead, it will be one of the many pin-point islands in the area. A special one called Das Island."

Crayle couldn't pass up the flip retort. "Is it German?"

"Ah, the American humor. We must mop up our operation forthwith, and send our settler friend on his way."

"Our humor, may I remind you, is evolved from yours."

"Anticipating your next question, no, we are not going to blow up the oil and gas terminal there. Bankrupting the Emirads is not our goal. The Emirates, as you likely know, were begun by Britain and are quite good friends of both our countries."

"Yes. There was a time when you Brits made friends all over the world."

"I believe you speak of India. Can you believe those bloody wogs? Wouldn't give up bugs for bangers."

"They needed that crunch. Your sausages just didn't have it."

"There's one other feature of this craft I forgot to mention, Mr. Crayle. Come on, everyone. Down below."

They followed their leader, then assisted him in battening down the hatches and portholes.

Matthew provided the command. "Take 'er down!"

Crayle's eyes went wide.

The Dhow began to sink.

He raced for the hatch in the overhead. Open it up. Get back up on deck.

Luke and Jane grabbed him.

"It's okay, mate," she told him in a calming, soft voice. " 'ere." She pointed to an archaic arm chair. " 'ave a sit."

The boat descended to thirty feet. Matthew pulled down the control end of a periscope, and peered in.

The operational piece sat high on the mast, and could manage 360 degrees visibility through its cylindrical, glass enclosure.

"What? You're going to arrive, surface, and pull up on a beach?"

"You shall see, my friend. In three hours. Get some sleep. We'll wake you in plenty of time."

Crayle stretched out on a wooden bench along the port side, and was out like a light.

• • •

Crayle came awake as Matthew had predicted. He took a look around. The portholes were unobstructed now. He watched as many of the ubiquitous Gulf fish glanced inside, as if to determine the nature of this strange fish, and see if there might be an available snack.

The boat rose and, as the water level outside processed down the portholes, Crayle felt something new.

"Wheels?"

A smile from apostle Luke.

"So, a boat ramp?"

With the time available, Luke thought he'd add to his cohorts base of knowledge. "This sucker has more to it than all the armaments I listed when we embarked. Retractable wheels."

"Not the standard off-the-shelf Dhow, is it?"

The others let Crayle's rhetorical slide. So he continued the thought.

"But the various navies of the Gulf have been tracking us the whole way. We're likely to be blown sky high shortly, armaments or no!" He started to do something, but didn't know what.

Matthew consoled him with additional intel. "This Dhow was built with switch-on/switch-off stealth technology. Works on the surface, under water, and even on land, except for visuals, of course."

"A genius of engineering I can appreciate, gentlemen …" He nodded to Jane. "… and lady."

As the boat moved along, the team of five went topside with their gear. Crayle noticed he was the only one with a firearm at the ready.

Mark passed out gas masks as they trouped down a gangplank.

Ashore, Crayle peered around the island. Individual buildings and pipes and fixtures galore, all shrouded in a white fog reminiscent of Dubai.

"This island is too small—a 1.21 kilometer by 2.4 kilometer rectangle—to have sand storms."

"That's three-quarters mile by one-and-a-half mile American," Crayle calculated.

"In colonial terms, yes. But you know I suppose they could blame Qatar, just to the West, but, no. It's a special concoction from your very own Science and Technology Directorate. All of the employees here are fast asleep. We'll be long gone before they revive. Come, Mr. Crayle. Let me show you around."

• • •

The assault team consisting of Magus Crayle and his four Apostles spread out. They slowly proceeded toward the small island's lone building. All manner of pipes, valves, and other petroleum handling ware indicated the nature and purpose of Das Island.

The lone enclosed facility appeared precisely as the Brit team's intel specified. A four-sided, single-story structure with two opposite sides flat, and the other two arcing outward. Whatever its actual physical underpinnings, the architectural style spoke of ancient Araby.

Though there were no human sounds or barking dogs or other non-natural indications of life, hopefully due to the sleep-inducing aerosol delivered earlier, the team remained ever alert to even slight danger in their *in situ* environment.

Prearranged, Mark and Luke circled the periphery of the structure clockwise. The newer American satellites had 'gone green' and provided high definition night vision. With their real time feed, they already knew there was no one outside. But, old habits die hard.

The pair completed its circumference surveillance and approached the others from the right. Both sported a thumbs up.

Gathered before the gold and highly ornate double door, weapons ready, Matthew and Jane gave a tug on the iron handles.

Surprise.

They opened.

Crayle led the squad inside.

The lights were full on, but evinced no one upright, seated, or in motion. Probably ten men lay prostrate in various spaces on the floor. None appeared to be at stations, so they'd had a few seconds to react to the drug before collapsing.

Jane, a former medic, tested all for life signs.

All good.

Crayle observed that each of the bulged out sides, to his left and right, had heavy duty, windowless steel doors. With padlocks.

He gave Jane a nod. He'd noticed on the Dhow she'd attached long, gray, plastic hair clips before donning her balaclava. He guessed the rest.

She stepped to the right hand door, removed a clip, and attached it to the lock. The operation was repeated on the left door.

Crayle still had no idea what this op was all about. In such a situation, it's difficult to know when you're done. Perhaps, one of the Apostles would so indicate.

Stepping back to the center, Jane primed her Smartphone, then looked to Crayle.

No better time, he thought.

Weapons at the ready.

He nodded.

Pop!

Pop!

They were ready for whatever happened next.

At least, that's what they thought.

CHAPTER 33

That the individual who staggered out through the left door was obviously conscious and unaffected by the room's air quality, indicated it could be safe for the team to remove their gas masks. They did.

Crayle absolutely gasped.

"Living Hell!" blasted into the room. "One living Hell!"

His hand slapped to his mouth.

"Oh. Hi, Mag."

"Hi, Mag? Hi, Mag? I've just blundered into a scene from *The Night of the Living Dead*. My God. How …"

The blonde, who'd just strayed into the room, began, "I can see why you might be mad, Mag. But we've been held incommunicado, as they say."

"You used 'we' … other prisoners? Here?"

"Not by choice. Oh, and the zombie reference." The blonde twirled the short, braided length of hair that hung by her left temple. A tribute to her long-deceased father. "About that hotel in Louisville.

Micmac had gotten me to wear a Hollywood style bullet-proof vest. It sprayed fake blood when I was hit. That Pattie chick was a good shot. Knocked me unconscious. After she left, the cleanup crew she summoned got me out of there and took me to the *dismantling* safe house. Some of them died after I woke up. Then, someone from behind. One of those Dial-A-Dose needles. Back to sleep."

"Phoebe, how'd you end up in the United Arab Emirates?"

"Bad karma, I guess."

"That whole thing in Louisville was more than bad karma."

"Turns out, my boss at the FBI was bad. Like Neil Wohlford. Illuminé. Set me up."

"You didn't hear?"

"Hear what?"

"They found him. Perforated. A spear gun projectile did the trick. Right through the heart."

She smiled. "Micmac. Hey, where is my main man, anyway?"

CHAPTER 34

"Phoebe, your main man is operational right now."

She didn't seem to hear. She'd motioned behind him.

In situations like these, he could turn just in time to watch an assassin fire a bullet. One he might not even hear.

He turned.

What he saw stopped him dead. Figuratively.

She nodded at Lenny. "I've almost killed him several times."

The former private investigator and team member stepped up next to Phoebe.

"Yeah. With malice aforethought, I might add."

Crayle closed the separation to the man, and grasped him tightly by both shoulders.

Then, his hands jumped to the man's throat. But Crayle's fingers wouldn't close.

The hands dropped. He stepped back.

"Jeez-Louise! You'd think … you'd think … "

"You're dead! You're a fine mist in the sky over Mecca! My God!"

"You can call me Lenny."

Again he clasped the shoulders. "How …"

"If you give me a little space." The diminutive man pressed his palms gently against Crayle's chest for emphasis.

Crayle caught his breath, then took a step back. "You blew up. You somehow ran off with one of our jets, and took that bomb with you. The mini-nuke you confiscated in Auckland. New Zealand. At the rugby match."

"Long story long. In Paris for the Lalumière coronation, I ran into Pope Whatshisname."

"Ran into?"

"Yeah. At the Notre Dame Cathedral. Turns out he'd lost his ride back to the Vatican. I thought he could give me a little boost up the ladder when my time came. So, I offered a ride."

"You're Jewish."

"Couldn't hurt."

"And the bomb?"

"Didn't want to leave it in the hotel room. I tossed it into my 'go' bag—the backpack. Along with some other things."

"Such as Micmac's remote control for the jets?"

"I had some room. Why not?"

"And customs had no problem? Your usual Walther PPK and an atomic bomb, made to look like a rugby ball?"

"Pope and his crew didn't get checked."

"And from there."

"Seems he had a gig in Jerusalem. I took him. You'll like this. Got to meet with him, the Israeli leader, and some Mossad dude."

"Mossad?"

"That's where I heard about an imminent missile attack from Iran. You know, Alona always said I should do something with my life. Something not selfish. So, off I went."

"To somehow intercept a nuclear-tipped missile bound for Israel."

"Something like that."

"From what we saw on the computer screen in Paris, the explosion and bright light high above Mecca—the actual target—you destroyed the missile. What am I missing?"

"I set the timer, and grabbed a parachute."

"You've never jumped before."

"It had 'easy opening' instructions. Slow jet down, open door, jump. When clear, pull 'D' Ring."

"You'd better not be making this up, Lenny."

"Would I lie to you?"

"Well …"

"Okay. Okay. Forget those times. This is straight up. You fall pretty fast when you jump from a plane."

"About 120 miles per hour, top speed. And that's unassisted by the speed of the plane."

"Yeah. It got my attention. But here's where I thought like you. The mathematician. The enemy missile would go way up in its arc, then come down. So, I'd positioned the 'THIS SIDE TOWARD THE ENEMY' side of the bomb facing up."

"It was one of the directional nukes, then."

"Yeah. Oh, and I grabbed Micmac's remote piloting rig. Way cool. After I punched out the chute, I made a couple of moves. That's when it happened."

"Whew. That's a lot for me to consume and digest."

"So, when it blew, the force, most of it, went up and destroyed the incoming bogie. The missile. The little bit of side and bottom blast—our musician friend, Micmac, would call the pattern cardioid—hit my sorry ass like a ton of bricks. The force shredded my chute. I was almost a big splash in that Mecca mosque. I managed the reserve chute just in time."

"That's beyond amazing, Lenny. Then, what?"

"I landed on this big black cube. The religious folks thought the boom and bright light and me were a sign. They took me away. To protect me. I thought it wise not to tell them I'm Jewish."

"As long as you weren't taking a public shower, you were good."

"Right. Then, they transported me to another sacred place, and you won't guess who I ran into there."

"Who, Lenny? Who?"

"Whine."

CHAPTER 35

Phoebe ignored Lenny and looked about. "Where is everyone? This is the distribution location for oil and gas loading. For the Emirates. There's usually a bunch of armed guards protecting this place. And the whole, so-called downstream operation. And the others getting the stuff loaded on ships."

They heard a commotion outside.

Closest to the front door, Crayle moved there, and switched off the lighting master.

He peeped out the door.

The facility's external flood lights pointed toward the bare ground and waterfront told all.

A military hovercraft had pulled onto the land and settled.

Crayle shut the door.

He whispered, though the hovercraft crew couldn't have heard him even at full volume.

"Three Tangos on a military float craft. Two gunners and a pilot. Mounted guns look like 7.62 millimeter. Full auto."

"Did they appear belligerent," Luke asked.

"Looks like a patrol. They've seen the Dhow sitting up on land and on its wheels. That's got their attention."

"I'll go out and 'ave a chat. My Arabic's bloody good."

Crayle stepped away from the door and stopped Mark with a hand to the chest.

"We all have silenced weapons. My call. We're taking them down. Before they can radio an alarm."

Unknown to him in the interior's darkened state, someone had slipped behind him.

A silenced .45 still makes some noise.

Phoebe, now outside the door, made three.

"Tangos down. Hard," she peeked inside and advised.

Led by Crayle with weapons at the ready, they all trooped through the door, and fanned out to either side of Phoebe.

Using techniques they knew too well, the Apostles assured that there were indeed three Tangos, and that they were all down. Hard. One bullet each. Between the eyes. Phoebe's trademark.

Crayle approached and boarded the craft.

The flood lights lit up the control panel, so he was able to deduce, despite the labeling in Arabic, which control was which.

He fired up the engine, lifting the boat off the ground.

Then, he spun it toward the sea.

At that point, he engaged the throttle lightly forward, and dove off the side as it departed.

With the craft just about 50 feet out, he turned to Phoebe.

He'd noticed she had somehow acquired an exact match for her former service weapon of choice, a .45 caliber Glock 30. Plus a silencer and a ten-shot, extended clip.

He nodded toward the departing watercraft.

Phoebe took aim, and emptied the remaining seven slugs into the craft's air surround.

Slowly, it decelerated and descended into the Gulf waters until the engine died. And then, the deep six.

"We're done here," Crayle announced to the team.

The Apostles headed for the Dhow with Lenny in tow.

Crayle turned to Phoebe with a quizzical look.

She read it.

"They knew about me. They brought the Glock here to enhance their torture experience."

He clasped her shoulders. "I'm sorry."

He noticed the welling up of tears in her eyes.

"They poked it in here." She pointed to her mouth. "… and then …"

He pulled her tight to him, then led her in following the others.

He knew they'd be away and submerged within about ten minutes.

As the ever vigilant, seven-person entourage padded toward the special Dhow, Crayle moved off to one side, out of earshot, and fetched a familiar device from his black cargo shorts.

CHAPTER 36

"Hekka," Crayle said into his phone. "Sorry for the mystery tonight. I'll fill you in when I see you."

"What, a sitrep?" She said it in a manner implying she perceived some sort of operation had occurred.

"Uh, if you don't mind, I need you to do a little something for me."

"Of course."

"I knew you'd understand. Pack up our things, and check out."

"What?"

"It's okay. A bellman can help with the baggage. Take a cab to ..." He gave her the destination. "Use this name." He supplied that. "You'll find the appropriate passport in the zipper side of my suitcase."

Hekka was beside herself. She felt as if she'd spent the past couple of minutes tumbling about in an industrial strength clothes dryer.

But, resolved, and with her head back in focus, she told him, "See you there, Magus." A pause. "We need to talk." She hung up.

• • •

When Hekka arrived at Dubai's version of the Atlantis Hotel, it's architectural beauty, pink color, and prominence at the top of the Jumeirah Palm took her breath away. She'd seen pictures of its namesake property in the Bahamas, and had always wanted to go.

Inside, she processed in at the registration desk, where the clerk looked her up and down as if to say, "What's this manner of riff-raff doing in the property's top end Royal Bridge Suite?" And, "A woman, no less? By herself?"

A manager stepped up with a larger than life smile, shoving his subordinate behind him.

"Mrs. Bond. Mrs. Jimmie Bond. How nice. Let me personally escort you to your room. By the way, everything is covered by a Black Card, courtesy of a Mr. Fleming, so please enjoy all that we have to offer."

So, Jack Sommers' famous card. She scanned the overly sumptuous lobby for any sign of her husband. No luck. She reminded herself. They did need to talk.

When she, the manager, and the bellman reached the room in its private elevator, she realized it was the high crosspiece one saw from outside that tied the two wings of the hotel together. Inside, it seemed both ornate to the maximum, and large enough to invite 500 of your closest friends, with room left over.

She didn't require the manager-supplied 924 square meters or its American system equivalent. It was huge. One entered into an opulent lounge area, and then wandered through the three sumptuous bedrooms, the spa-like bathroom, and the 16 person formal dining area. The ceiling was so high, she couldn't reach it at three times her own height and on tiptoes.

Then the views. Out one side and down the famous Palm to Dubai proper, or in the other direction, northwest across The Gulf.

The manager cleared his throat. "Did I mention the twenty-four seven team of butlers, and the on-call chef?"

Perhaps she'd thought a little harshly of her husband. Perhaps this was the surprise he had in store for her to counter her surprise with the James Bond Island episode at Phuket.

She thanked the manager, supplied a generous tip for both men, and then smiled in the direction of the door. They left.

Hekka wandered about the Atlantis' premier room for several minutes when the front door opened.

There stood Magus Crayle, looking like a train wreck personified, smiling. "Honey, I'm ho-ome!"

His impression of the famous Desi Arnaz line brought on her minimalist smile. "What I want to hear is, *Honey, I'm done.*"

He took a couple of steps her way. "I've got a surprise."

"I see the surprise." She swept her extended hand horizontally across the room's panorama.

On cue, and in through the door to his left, entered the two people Hekka knew she'd never see again.

She stumbled backward, and unceremoniously dropping onto the couch behind her. At that point, one of the toughest and most resilient women on the planet crumbled.

Phoebe ran to sit at her side. Lenny took the other side.

The on-loan FBI agent pulled Hekka tight to her. Lenny wrapped his arms, too.

The sum total of it all had finally taken its toll.

Hekka sobbed.

CHAPTER 37

The flight from Dubai's DXB airport couldn't come soon enough. Crayle, Hekka, Phoebe, and Lenny said their goodbyes to the Apostles—Matthew, Mark, Luke, and Jane—knowing they just might run into them again.

He considered the wondrous achievement the Emirates had put forth, starting with the endless sand dunes of the Saudi Peninsula. He also considered writing a travel review for the mystical and extensive Atlantis Resort, the Dubai Marina, and the Al Murooj Hotel, with its platoon-sized balcony. The newspaper rack in its lobby brought him back to reality. The top newspaper was about 80% redacted. He'd never seen such a thing. Perhaps the CIA had a psy-ops unit in Dubai.

Pilot Marli had them wheels up in short order. Headed East on autopilot, she fixed everyone a stiff drink before returning to the flight deck. They all suspected she had a flask of her own hidden up there somewhere. She did. Fortunately, the autopilot plus new autoland feature had the helm, as Micmac would put it.

Finishing his drink, Crayle walked back to the bedroom. Time for a little snooze. He stopped. There on the bed facing him lay Phoebe fast asleep. Right behind was a sleeping Lenny, his arm draped over her. This wasn't going to end well if she awoke first.

He pictured her at the open rear, port-side door. With a firm grip on the diminutive P.I.

"Bye, Lenny! Hope you survive the bounce!"

Crayle gently removed the arm. He stepped back, then returned to his seat.

When he awoke in his reclined seat hours later, he noticed all three team members busily attending to iPad games. Spy games. Lenny appeared fine and well-rested, so had not repeated the infraction with Phoebe.

"Wheels down. Ten minutes," came Marli's voice over the intercom. "Hong Kong … land ho!"

The ensuing scramble had everyone ready to deplane as Jack Sommers' ex brought the Dassault Falcon 8X to a halt. The team trouped out with their pilot in the lead. The immigration officials each glanced at her neckline, smiled, and bowed. With zero scrutiny, the team's armaments never set off alarms or saw light of day.

A curious Crayle stepped up beside Marli to ask how the customs officers always knew to leave them alone. They had no photos and hadn't peered into phones or other devices.

"Left collar," she said.

There it was. A bright yellow happy face sticker. Yes, it was true. The CIA could move in strange ways.

But, that was it. Take predictable and shit can it, as Micmac would so eloquently say.

"*Crap!*" Crayle said out loud. Micmac still doesn't know.

He checked his phone. "*Crap!*" again. Still dark. He felt a hand on his arm.

"It's copasetic," Phoebe said. "I want to surprise him." She affected a sly smile. "And we'll need some serious privacy."

• • •

On the road to Empress Ling's palace, Crayle continuously monitored his phone. He smiled as he shook his head at the comms icon, a pair of zig-zag lightning bolts covered by a translucent, charcoal-colored cloud. It was not what he wanted to see.

• • •

The super stretch limo arrived atop Victoria Peak and passed through the palace gates. Ling, attired in her iconic black cheongsam dress, awaited the new entourage atop the front steps. Solid gold steps. A lucky number—odd other than nine, but eight, exceptionally lucky. There were eight. In accord with the Chinese culture.

The team formed up, placed their right fists in their left palms, and bowed deeply. Only Lenny got it wrong.

Ling's bow was a barely perceptible nod—apropos of her station. She turned and entered the palace.

The team trouped up the steps and followed the empress into the greeting hall.

Ling knew Lenny and Phoebe from before. The violent before. She also knew them to be dead. Her deadpan demeanor upon seeing them perfectly healthy perplexed Crayle. But, he reasoned, the Chinese could do that. Yet another book title came to mind. *The Chinese Enigma.*

No, he reconsidered. Redundant.

Ling directed them to take a seat on the red velvet and gold couches that faced a hallway. They admired, once again, the spectacular precious metal, ivory, and jade inlays on the floors and walls.

"I'll be right back," she said as she strode down the hallway.

In just a couple of minutes, the team heard footsteps echoed ever louder as Ling made her way back to them. She appeared first, then her hand holding another came into view. Then, Micmac.

He looked up, and stopped dead.

Phoebe stared first at him, and then at the hand he held. Her immediate take was that her husband and Ling had become an entity after her own apparent demise. Her jaw fell open in shock. At her loss. All her hopes raised high with her rescue in the Emirates, and amplified in transit, dashed.

Micmac's jaw was likewise disposed. Quick, he tugged at the handhold, but Ling's grip was too tight.

The empress led him across the hall and extended her arm, Micmac still attached, to Phoebe.

The on-loan FBI Agent slowly raised hers as Ling coupled the hands, and clasped them tightly with her own.

"You are one again," she said. "No more words required."

The two took turns moving their lips closer to the other.

Finally, they touched.

Micmac wrapped his arms around his wife so tight she let out a yelp.

• • •

Lenny watched the entire affair and thought of his own number one. Alona. What manner of reception could he expect? She might kill him for not letting her know he was alive. No, that wasn't it. It'd been a long time since she'd had sex. He glanced back at the MacKay embrace.

"*Whine.*"

• • •

A few minutes later, Ling intervened. "I have a room prepared. Please, follow me.

She led them off for some requisite private time, returning without them.

"We'll have some tea. Can you stay a few days?"

"I'm afraid we have to get back. I'd like for Phoebe and Micmac to stay, if that's okay. I have to get Lenny home, and then a little R & R for Hekka and myself."

"And after that, back to work? Why don't you retire? Live here at my palace. Rent free." She managed a brief laugh. "You each bring skills I desperately need, and my faith in you is without question."

"Trust me," Crayle responded. "It's a wonderful offer. I'll pose it to the president. First, though, I owe him some serious time back there in D.C."

And he did owe President Stones a renaissance of the CIA. A rebirth, as it was. That could take a couple of years. And then there was the Parsi and his three bombs over in India. And the remaining trio of mini-nuclear devices. Somewhere.

CHAPTER 38

Back from Hong Kong, Marli landed the Falcon 8X at Jack Sommers International Airport—its unofficial name—with Crayle, Hekka, and Lenny aboard. Their ride was ready and waiting, courtesy of the covert CIA hospital nearby.

The ambulance—packed to the brim with Mag Crayle, wife Hekka, and their luggage and souvenirs, plus Lenny—serpentined to the top of Highway 18 where they took the Stanfield Cutoff over the East end of Big Bear Lake to the 'downtown' aspect of the mountain resort valley and then to Boulder Bay. Crayle already felt at home as they passed The Iron Squirrel restaurant. At 2.3 miles West of town, they arrived at the tiny suburb, Boulder Bay, and the Lipschitz upscale log cabin home.

Out first, he stepped to the door, and rang the bell. Three times. A pause. Then twice.

"Come in! It's unlocked," came a shout from within.

Hekka stepped up beside her husband. She didn't want to miss the fireworks.

He hollered over his shoulder, "Get your ass in here!"

Out of the still-bewildered Alona's eyesight, she heard the response as its source stepped into view.

"Whine!"

Alona placed baby Lenny in a Jolly Jumper. She pulled her baby down to release him, heard Lenny, and ran toward the sound. The baby, still in the jumper, flew upward. She raced to the entryway. Ready to eliminate her better-off-dead husband into his component parts. It was as if he'd applied a firearm silencer to his ensuing exhortation, achieving impact at suppressed volume.

She stopped.

Tears flowed.

Lenny, who'd just made it to the front step, realized that he was supposed to have been the nuclear, aerial epicenter on the team's Dassault Falcon 7X over Mecca, Saudi Arabia. Should've been instantly vaporized.

They embraced as if in competition for the most severe hug.

"It's Christmas," Alona declared.

That she and her husband were Jewish mattered not.

"*It's blanking Christmas!*"

• • •

A few minutes later and minus Lenny, the ambulance transported the remaining two passengers West across the Big Bear Lake dam, then North toward home.

Crayle and Hekka peered out the vehicles one-way, bullet proof side window as they passed Micmac and Phoebe's cabin.

"They'll be back soon."

"The place looks different without the M1A1 Abrams tank in the front yard."

He heard a noise, and observed his phone. "Hey, the darkness is lifted. Comms enabled. Finally." He tapped on the screen. "I'm reviewing emails."

A minute passed.

"Check this out. Somehow President Stones got the MacKay's baby to Hong Kong!"

"Wow! I bet it's Flori. Kimbel would choose her to fly a baby halfway around the world. To its parents."

"Unless you have more emails, it means our baby is still in Washington … with the president."

"More likely with Susanna and Luisa."

"When they're not putting together speeches for him."

The ambulance rounded the northwest corner of Big Bear Lake, passed through the tiny village known as Fawnskin, and turned right into their cabin's driveway.

Their log cabin, the smaller of two on the property, looked every bit as it did when they left. Jack Sommer's 'big house' was off to their right with a garage halfway between.

Crayle schlepped the roller bags to the front door as Hekka punched in their code. While '007' didn't seem that unique, it served the purpose. Neither ever forgot.

"We can unpack later. I hope all the ceramic and colorful Aladdin's Lamps you bought in the Middle East as souvenirs survived the journey."

He headed for the refrigerator.

"Blue Moon Belgian?"

CHAPTER 39

Crayle and Hekka took it easy out on their back deck. They no longer had the gargantuan pine tree in the back yard thanks to a previous assault featuring bomb-carrying drones, but the late year, cool temperature eliminated the necessity for shade.

"So," Hekka began. "What do we get baby Kianna for her first birthday?"

"How about … a baby brother?" Crayle made a faux attempt at unbuckling his belt.

Hekka teased. "A boy? To protect her?"

"Protecting the procreator of the species is our sworn and necessary duty." He elevated his eyebrows added dramatic effect.

"I was thinking more along the lines of my ten-inch Bowie. For Kianna."

"Ten inches?"

"Perhaps four inches. A starter Bowie."

"You're right, Hekka. She could stay at home, and defend herself while her new brother goes off and studies math and physics."

She caught the slight, and glanced about. "Where *is* my Bowie?"

"Just kidding. Keep your knife in its scabbard, Pocahontas."

"If President Stones didn't need you so badly at the CIA, I might just send you off to the White Man's lesser version of the Happy Hunting Grounds."

"We call it Heaven."

"You've made your point though, Magus."

"What point?"

"That Lenny is the male team member with the sense of humor." A sly smile followed.

"Jeez-Louise," was the next sound they heard.

Lenny stomped out onto the back deck looking like a man with a mission. "The president can't get you on the phone, so he tasks me to come over and get you outta the shower."

Hekka responded. "We got wise. We turned our phones off."

"Let's have it," Crayle said.

"He needs you in D.C. Like yesterday. Stuff goin' on. Serious stuff."

"What stuff, Lenny? Details matter."

"I asked for details."

"And … "

"And he said I didn't have the Need To Know." Lenny performed a palms up and rising gesture. "Can you imagine?"

Both Crayle's shook their heads in mock disbelief.

"Well … well … whine! That's it. I'll whine … and then I'll whine some more."

"If you check behind you, Hekka has drawn her Bowie, and is thumbing the blade. To see if it's dull enough."

"Okay, okay. Just call him. Okay?"

"Yes, Lenny. I'll fire up my phone and hook up."

"Oh, and be sure to include me and Alona if there's something juicy. We miss the old team effort thing. Okay?"

Crayle's special Smartphone beeped as it achieved operational readiness. He glared at Lenny, who apparently intended to eavesdrop. "Need To Know?"

"Jeez-Louise," Lenny muttered as he stomped back through the cabin.

"President Stones," emanated from the comms device. Crayle put the phone to his ear.

"It's me."

"My phone indicates you've still been dark, though you're back in Big Bear. I'd hate to think you switched the damn thing off."

"Let's skip the accusatory repartee, Kimbel. I need to run inside and impregnate my wife. She's only receptive for short periods, pardon the pun."

He glanced at Hekka, smiling and seeking approval for his humor. His smile died. He blamed Lenny's brief presence for the bad joke.

"Need you here, Mag. Something big enough on the intel radar. I can't put it on the phone. Not even encrypted. Gotta be the STIF under Manassas."

"I'll need a plane."

"On the way. Flori expects to touch down in an hour. At Jack Sommers International down by the Quarry."

"One hour. That's not enough time for all the baby creating."

"If you're not there, my number one pilot has orders to come up the hill and fetch you. She's got enough of that Brazil-sexy charm that Hekka will soon whisk you on your way in self defense."

"Hekka has no worries about me and anyone else, but, okay. I'll pack light and take the Cobra. I'll get the covert EMT crew to the airport. They can store my car at the Quarry hospital until I return.

Now Hekka's eyebrows raised.

"Until *we* return."

"Done and done. See you in a few."

The president hung up.

CHAPTER 40

Later that day, Crayle and Stones sat facing one another, yet again, at the Manassas, Virginia underground STIF room. The former still groused that he had to make the porta-potty ingress, supplying the requisite short and curly for ID, while the president sailed to the site from D.C. on the 300 mph vacuum tunnel transport pod. Such was the privilege of rank.

"On paper, the Company is the most secret spy shop in the world." That was President Stones' set up. He glanced over at Crayle to take the hand off, and run from there.

"First of all, it's on paper. Therefore, it's not a secret. I'll give you my CIA remake. I've given it massive thought in between all the operations and equally massive attempts on my life. Here goes.

"No more CIA-labeled goods. No ball caps. No T-shirts. No branding. In short, no tangible anything to connect our people to the Company.

"No bureaucratic names. Director of Clandestine Services—gone. Director of CIA back to DCI. First directorate returns to DO headed by a Director of Operations. Et cetera.

"Directorate 2, Science and Technology. We keep the link to Micmac for the new and wild spy tools he comes up with. Third directorate: Analysis headed by a Director of Analysis, or DA, with a DDA as backup.

"We'll modularize so cyber attacks leave unaffected groups intact.

"We go back to country-designated desks as before where members have to know the geography, economy, government, people and their culture, current status and future projections, strong suits, and weaknesses, should we need to exploit them.

"Keep major arm's length from Congress. And we'll need FBI liaison with that. We have to know if troublemakers have radical domestic allegiance, or are dialed in to foreign governments or non-state actors."

"Wait a second. You know we can't control Congress—separation of something or other. Right?"

"We keep with the 'no ops within the U.S.' while quietly handling necessities with the Strategic Solutions Office—Jack's group."

"We go off-the-books, then, in messing with the congressional assholes."

"I was trying not to get technical."

"I shouldn't use that characterization, but they swear to do for *We The People*, then go off into their insular, narcissistic, political world, and either set up roadblocks or extort absurd line items in return for doing what it is their duty to do." Stones, an optimist, tried to avoid the *Swamp* topic. It always upset him about the D.C. players.

"It upsets you, because you are not one of the players here. No getting weathered in and desensitized in the House, Senate, or a state capitol."

"Right again, Magus."

"Moving along, I'll implement at the CIA a government version of the ISO 9000 family of standards. Nothing but quality. Of course, the specific ISO 9001 Quality Management implementation may require an independent certification body to ensure conformity with the standards. Our target is the best HUMINT, SIGINT, and IMINT on the planet."

"Hold on. An International Standards Organization approach to quality?"

"It works in private industry."

"Might work at the Company if it weren't for all those classified restrictions."

"Fortunately, they allow for us to perform our own audits. With internal sub-audits along the way. To keep us on track."

"Anything else?"

"Gap analysis."

"Enough of the esoterica. I'll just have to trust you."

"How'd things work at the NSA when you were there? Before you became vice president?"

"Well, my boss would sit me down and read me in on a new project. Like the one on the Diomede Islands. I asked if my security clearance level was high enough." He stopped. "Wait a minute." He sat back, fingers interlaced. "I'm not sure, Mag, you have the Need To Know for this."

"Oh, we're going to play. I'm not sure you need me as the new CIA chief."

"Uncle, uncle, uncle. Alright. My boss said he couldn't read me in if I didn't have the necessary clearance and Need To Know. Then, he read me in."

"Your mind put it together. You knew by his read in that you possessed the necessary tickets."

"*Voilà!*"

"That's pretty sharp for an NSA operative, Mr. President."

"Okay, okay. You're on the right track regarding the CIA post. Get the *Devil In The Details* down so we get our premier spook agency back into the shadows. And no leaks to the press, or Congress, or God on any of this."

"When I'm done lecturing, they'll understand the legal term, Sedition. And its consequences."

"A capital crime, if I'm not mistaken."

"Subversion of the government. I'll add the responsibility for carrying out the sentence to Jack and his crew."

"Which brings us to your team probably riding off into the sunset."

"We're all at a good stopping point. It's time."

President Stones nodded.

Crayle dropped into deep thought of the monumental change ahead. He considered time with Hekka, baby Kianna, and their newly unencumbered friends. Lenny might go back to private investigating. Alona to her profession as defense counsel. Phoebe back to witness protection at the FBI. Micmac inventing for the Science and Technology director.

The president's voice brought him back to the present.

"Oh, Magus, there's just one more thing."

"Swell."

"I have something new coming up. Called Operation Blue Sky. I want you to—"

"Facilitate. Yeah, I've run blue sky sessions before. Get a bunch of people together, who might hate each others' guts, and put out ideas to consider. Take in disparate and conflicting ideas, while ensuring that none of them are rejected out of hand. So, you'll let me know … when?"

"Oh, later. Not a big deal. Hey, I believe you have a plane to catch."

CHAPTER 41

Czarina Anastasia Romanov considered leaving her chief advisor and confidant, Raspi, behind. He'd proven himself more than capable of handling affairs at Catherine Palace near St. Petersburg. He would use his magic to detect budding intrigues and extinguish them in short order.

No, she'd take him with her to Moscow. They'd already tousled regarding the mode of transportation. He wanted the one hour twenty-five minute flight from Pulkovo airport to Sheremetyevo via their Sukhoi-Gulfstream S-21 supersonic, with a definite space-age appearance, business jet. Quick over. Quick back.

She, on the other hand, chose her newly created replica czarist-era train. Fast, smooth, and with creature comforts befitting her royal station. The vehicles sported so much in gold embellishments, special mega-duty suspensions had to be fabricated in Germany. The transit, she was informed, would take precisely three hours and forty-five minutes. As fast as the high-speed SAPSAN.

Her special adjoining car contained a full wardrobe. She could select attire according to her mood. And there was the special gown in black, expressing her deep mourning for the deceased Vladimir. And its ultra-special, elastic midriff. She would say nothing, but others would notice a bulge there. Surely, they would say nothing at the time, lest they be accused of implying the czarina was gaining weight. Not an issue over which to lose one's head.

Once aboard, Raspi assured they were alone in the car before he spoke. "It is quite ingenious, your offer to the presidium to deliver Vlad's body to Moscow, and place it next to the other Vlad in that one's tomb."

"Are you familiar with the English word, sycophant?"

"Of course. I speak well the English. It means a kissing of asses."

"It's a negative term, Raspi."

"But I love kissing your ass."

At that, she stood and removed her clothes.

"We have a surfeit of time before we arrive in Moscow. Kiss all that you dare."

• • •

The czarina's train chugged into Moscow precisely on time. The views from the czarina's special car were magnificent. Lots and lots of Russian snow.

Raspi wished there weren't windows in the bedroom so he could have at least respite from the czarina's insatiable amorous appetite.

Finally, though, they arrived at Kiyevsky Station near the town center. By the time they stepped outside, a military unit fired the traditional twenty-one gun salute.

Reporters with cameras worked into position to catch a side shot. One that showed the curve of an imperial baby inside.

Finally, as she and Raspi had scripted, she posed, raising her arms.

The crowd went wild.

She brought her hands down to rub the prospective future leader of the New Russian Empire.

"It's a boy," she said in Russian.

It was hard to say which made more noise, the applause or the cameras.

Porters brought along for the occasion moved Vladimir's coffin out onto an Eighteenth Century wagon drawn by four horses instead of two. The amount of gold on the wagon and coffin made the extra pair necessary. After a security inspection to assure that Vladimir and only Vladimir occupied the box, the caisson moved out.

At Lenin's Tomb, the porters transferred the coffin inside and placed it next to Russia's first Communist dictator. The eponymous Vladimir Lenin had ruled from 1917 to 1924, to be replaced by Alexei Rykov.

The czarina addressed the throng.

She began by telling them she'd be in Moscow for a few days, but right now needed a moment alone with the two Vladimirs. After much nodding by the attendees, she entered the tomb. Raspi closed the door behind her.

The crowd hushed at first, going wild when she finished and stepped back outside the tomb. They missed the part inside where she pulled the mini-nuke bomb from concealment against her belly, and put it into Vladimir's coffin. She'd locked it, then disappeared the sole key into her bra. An inflatable bladder, just the size of the bomb, replaced the bomb to maintain *the look*.

Back outside, she glanced around at the attendees, taking their measure.

Those who'd pushed to the front were the Communist elite. Since Vladimir had been one, he couldn't bring himself to terminate them and their lethal potential when he declared himself czar not long ago.

For that reason, as well as their fanatical adherence to extreme left principles, they represented the most lethal threat to her reign as Czarina of the Russian Empire.

Her mind had sorted it out. She knew what she needed to say.

"My countrymen. Welcome."

No applause. Just silence

"Vladimir would've preferred to address you himself, but as you can see, he is permanently indisposed."

Now, anger began to capture the front row's histrionics. She needed them upset to excess by the time she finished.

"As you are well aware, Vladimir was a life-long, devoted Communist. For him to abandon the extreme left ideology required a monumental realization. One I was able to instill only after utilizing my own humble, world-class skills of persuasion."

It was working. Faces in front turned red, ready to burst. She noticed several individuals speaking into their shirt cuffs, summoning all adherents.

If she had it right, they'd form a confab after she departed. With closed doors and no windows, they'd conspire to overthrow the czarina and seize control. Bolshevism would be back. And in full control.

"The previous notable Vladimir, Ulyanov, took the pseudonym, Lenin. He was likewise a fool. The proletariat would overthrow the blood-elected czar, and rule for the working class."

She smiled. Heads appeared on the verge of exploding.

It would take just a few hours for the masses to descend upon the Lenin mausoleum. By then, she'd be safely away.

"Of course, my Vladimir's hero, Lenin, received his college degree from my hometown's University of Saint Petersburg. There, he completed exams externally. That means others wrote them on his behalf. A disgrace. For that reason, I hereby rename his birth city from Ulyanovsk back to its original Simbirsk."

The Communists were ready to riot. Raspi's guard unit, replete with automatic weapons at the ready and seeming out of place at a eulogy, precluded any moves that threatened the czarina. All the better for their emotions to fester.

"And in conclusion, my Vladimir shall rest aside his namesake for eternity—however long that is. Please pay your respects here for at least the next 24 hours. Here, in the tomb of the two Vladimirs."

She could tell the Marxist-Leninist faithful heard none of her last utterances. They'd already set in motion a plot. A two-pronged plot. First, to bring loyal forces to Moscow's Red Square to honor the Vlads. Second, to execute the czarina and prospective future czar in public, thus taking control of the new Russian Empire.

They'd declare the Second Coming of the Soviet Union, break out the hammer-and-sickle flags, kept neatly folded in a climate-controlled warehouse in Ulyanovsk. The birthplace of Lenin.

She had, via Raspi, real-time intel from an espionage asset among the comrades. All suspicions confirmed.

"It is time for a Vladimir moment. All close your eyes, and pray if you can. For Vladimir."

She knew the Communists, atheists all, could not pray. And that she'd just stuck a finger in their collective eye for the final time. They did comply with the eye closure, though.

When they opened them, the czarina had vanished.

With all festivities complete, she, Raspi, and her entourage returned to the train. The bulk of the crowd had shown its immense respect, but she'd also noticed more than several individuals wearing that traditional, blank Russian stare, expressing without words their belief that the seat of government really belonged in Moscow, not way out West in Saint Petersburg.

• • •

Far from the old capitol in her private car with Raspi, she enjoyed to the fullest her pending victory, *in flagrante*. She was reaching a climax and ready to press the button for the bomb … and her phone rang.

Magus Crayle. By the time she finished with him, she'd travelled out of range for the remote.

"*Chiort vozni*!"

Damn!

CHAPTER 42

The Parsi sat in his living room with his wife. She could tell he was having a stressful, personal moment.

"Did I do the right thing?" He worried in his native Persian. Instead of relaxing back in his sumptuous, embroidered chair, he sat at its front edge. Elbows on knees. Hands to face.

"Why do you always fret in the language of your ancestors? Worry in Portuguese so I can comfort you."

Rustom knew his wife was right. He did need comfort. He'd acquired three mini-nuke devices for his re-conquest of his mother country, Persia. But, in conversing with the American spy—the genius Crayle—he'd bargained away one of the bombs.

"You did what you thought best. You secreted the rugby ball-like weapon into Iran, using the coastal smugglers route you discussed with him. I still don't know how you got it past the border guards at Bandar Beheshti."

"Money talks. In all languages. And telling them that it was a gift for their friend, the Grand Ayatollah leader. Very secret."

"And explosive. Was that Mr. Crayle's idea?"

"I'd like to take credit, but yes. His idea."

"Then to Tehran, where you managed it into Russian Czar Vladimir's coffin. To be shipped to Saint Petersburg."

"The czarina has transported it to Moscow. Somehow, she'd get the old line Communists, plotting to overthrow her congregated in Red Square."

"A great plan. They'd have to come to celebrate the most notable of their own. The other Vladimir, Lenin, was surely that."

"That tactic also has the smell of Crayle about it."

"It's a miracle you didn't kill him when you had him here."

"I'll need more than a miracle to oust the Islamist usurpers of my Persia."

"Good to have the Miracle Man on your side, then."

"Yes."

"What did the czarina promise you in return for the bomb, darling? Was it sex?"

He looked up. "Sex? Why … uh … actually … she did. How did you know? Or was it a lucky guess?"

"Czarina Anastasia is known for her sexual proclivities. Her lust for power and sex are innate. Whether it's all the people of Russia, or just one mere man. Insatiable, I've heard."

"*Mere*, am I?"

"It was humor. I will have to master the Persian language, and deliver my jokes to you so you can get them."

"Since you shall become my queen, yes, you must learn Persian. And Arabic, as well."

She picked up the TV remote. "I'll get right on that."

"Anyway, she will assist in any way I deem necessary toward my conquest of Iran. Russia has beaucoup officials, military, and spy operations *in country*. It's just get the leaders together and *boom, boom*. Out go the lights … for them."

"So, we wait."

"Yes. We wait."

CHAPTER 43

The locale selected for the very special summit meeting was the Portuguese island of Madeira situated in the Atlantic Ocean, about 250 miles west of the Moroccan coast. The hotel chosen for the event was arranged to be completely empty save carefully vetted staff.

The architectural crafting of the property's three tall wings, appearing from above like an angular, ocean-facing parenthesis, cradled the two large pools and pool bar. Situated just over six miles down the island's east coast from Aeroporto da Madeira and eight miles east of the capital city, Funchal, its location provided its guests with a comfortable and safe respite from the rigors and formalities of their own royal palaces.

The three private jets made a required penultimate stop in Lisbon before the final one and three-quarter hours leg. The Crayle's Dassault Falcon had transported them to Lisbon from Dulles International near Washington, D.C., and their meet with the president, in just under six and a half hours. Crayle relaxed the team with 'this is going to be fun' despite the nobility in attendance.

A man looking a lot like Jack Sommers met them out front of the hotel and hustled them inside past men and women security guards sporting automatic weapons. He deposited them in the appropriate room, then disappeared. It appeared that all arrivals were quite well synchronized.

Not at all a woman with a weak constitution or lack of self-confidence, Hekka noted that the three women who'd just made an entrance could challenge her.

The first, the Queen of Sweden, entered the main ballroom of Hotel Riu Palace Madeira on the arm of Jean-Marc Lalumière, a.k.a. King Louis XX of France. The blond hair descending from her crown appeared to be made of platinum spun into fine shoulder-length strands by a royal spider. And yes, what a fine web she could weave.

Hekka possessed a sense for such from her own Serrano Indian heritage. When the queen gazed at Jean-Marc, it was clear she was a one man woman.

The Czarina of the new Imperial Russia, passing second, was voluptuousness at its worst. She met eyes with every man in the room, as if sequencing them for bedtime later on. All of them. And, as if to taunt Hekka, her eyes lingered that extra second when they met Crayle's. The B-word came to mind.

The final challenge entered last. Ling, Empress of China. The men in the room were protected from her perfect figure by the red, green, and gold cloak of her ultimate station. As she passed Crayle, she doffed it and handed it to him as their eyes met. Underneath, she wore the black silk cheongsam dress, slits up both sides, with the gold embellishments she, like the other of China Yao-wu's orphan 'daughters', earned on the arrival of their eighteenth birthdays. The tight neck of the dress served to perch a perfect face and present her renowned rounded lips, which always seemed to offer themselves for some purpose or other.

"Hekka!"

Crayle repeated the whispered imperative.

"*Hekka!*"

"Oh, yes. Welcome to you all!"

Her husband stepped forward. “All. Please be seated. The entourages must deploy to the outer chambers, due to the high level of the talks. Mr. Lipschitz will show you the way.”

Lenny proceeded to hustle the security details through doors held open by Micmac and Phoebe. The diminutive P.I. managed to divert their focus from their charges to himself. Is he a threat, or a just a formidable pest they wondered.

The meeting was now down to the principals. Crayle started the summit.

“I represent the United States. The document you are now receiving from Lenny, Alona, Micmac, and Phoebe bear the president’s signature, and affords me with plenipotentiary powers. In a word, I can sign any agreements made in this auspicious summit, thereby committing the full faith, et cetera, of the United States of America.”

The czarina couldn’t resist. “You could write a check from your treasury?”

“I could.” He tapped his coat with his hands, affecting a puzzled look. “I seem to have forgotten the check book. But let’s get down to business. We have America, France, Russia, and China present to deal once and for all with the subject of the miniature nuclear devices that have ravaged many nations. A toast then, to our most necessary success.”

The king and queen clinked, then took initial sips of the ’82 Dom Perignon provided. For the czarina, it was a mix of *Russkiy Standart* and *Stolichnaya* vodkas. Crayle surprised Ling with a vintage bottle of wine from the region he and Micmac had destroyed when they’d caused the nuclear bombs in the Chinese factory to self-detonate.

“Before we begin, a second toast. To our good friend, Empress Ling, on her 21st birthday! She must depart in a few hours, so I intend to facilitate this meeting and make it as efficient as possible.”

He led them in a rendition of Happy Birthday, which produced a confluent cacophony of English, Russian, French, and Chinese accents.

The czarina spoke first. "As your CIA estimates are so accurate, you are aware we have enough nuclear weapons of our own such that six percent could take care of business."

"Make the planet barren."

"Yes. *Byesplodniy*. Barren. As you are also aware, I am bringing back the religion to my Russia that the atheist Communists sought to destroy. Vladimir is gone now, along with his goons. And since the way forward is so filled with multitudes of pathways … it should have a name … ah … "

"*Yevangeliya Labirint*," he proposed.

"The Gospel Labyrinth. Your Russian accent is excellent, Mr. Crayle."

"Thank you. I'll have to save that one for a future novel."

Czarina Anastasia raised her hand. "We must be efficient today for another reason, Magus … uh … Mr. Crayle." She threw a quick glance at Hekka. "I must get back today also. Tomorrow, I replace my dear, late Vladimir's non-god religious tenor with a return to the Russian Orthodox Church. With my religion. I shall be present at the Church of the Savior on Spilled Blood for services. I'm sure all of you will understand. Even you, Jean-Marc, a devoted atheist, who recently received your crown in, let me see, was it the renovated Notre Dame Cathedral?" She didn't wait. "Yes. From Cardinal … what was his name? *Eh. Oui*. Richelieu. A descendant of the original. Hmmm?"

Jean-Marc took the bait. "At least I didn't sleep with him … not to mention your Rasputin descendant. The one you call Raspi."

Crayle jumped in. "All right. Let's get to it. Empress Ling. The current status of miniature nuke production in China."

Ling stood, executing a brief bow to the others. "I am honored. The status is that no more bombs can be made. The explosion destroyed the factory, all schematic materials, and every scientist involved. Attempts to revive the capability will meet with extreme prejudice as Magus … Mr. Crayle might articulate." She didn't sink to the czarina's taunt level by glancing at Hekka. "There is bad news, I'm afraid."

The last line produced a hush. They were talking nuclear devices, not fireworks.

"There are six bombs outstanding."

That pronouncement elicited another hush. No one would indicate they knew, even if they did. The czarina had one she'd just delivered to Moscow. That left five. Crayle knew about Rustom's three. But not that one of them was the czarina's.

Ling continued. "The records of distribution went up with the bomb factory. As you would guess, there were no duplicates."

Crayle responded. "Then I take it upon myself to track down each one, and see that they bring no harm. You'll all note that the bombs have been deployed expressly to change the political landscape. Our research has tracked the global Illuminé plot to something they called The Blackstone Strategy."

Ling produced the classic Asian inscrutability to perfection. She recalled clearly her early days with her adoptive father, stock market mogul and later the first Chinese emperor since Ch'in Xihuangdi. Crayle spent two years in Hong Kong developing the aforementioned strategy. His presence produced her first inkling of what love felt like. And the devastation of the English language term, unrequited.

Still, sans expression, she listened.

"It was that Blackstone Strategy that enabled France's return to monarchy," Jean-Marc informed those assembled. "I have what I wanted, and shall no longer support future upheavals, but shall fully support the friend of all that is France, Magus Crayle, in his quest."

"We're done, then," their host announced. "At least, the three of you are. It's all on me now. I'll keep you informed. When we meet again via secure comms, I hope it's to announce that all six mini-nukes have been destroyed."

Ling and Jean-Marc nodded.

The czarina raised her hand to attract Crayle's attention.

"I do have to depart." She smiled at the others, then turned back to Crayle. "Could I have a moment … in private?"

CHAPTER 44

Czarina Anastasia Romanova wasted no time returning home from the summit. She'd had the private moment with Crayle she needed—although not the one she desired—and was ready to implement. She needed her noble assistant's help and decided to turn his attitude positive. In the royal bedroom.

"We need to get you on our jet."

"We?"

"Royal plural."

"Of course."

"Enough of that. I need you to take this ..." She pulled a limited functionality version of the CIA Universal Remote Crayle'd given her in private from beneath the pillow. "There's a gathering today at Lenin's mausoleum in Moscow, a large one, to pay respects to the two Vladimirs. All of my enemies will be there. You'll fly our jet to Domodedovo Airport, South of Moscow center, not the usual Sheremetyevo on the North side. While the pilot refuels, you goof off."

Raspi pinched his eyebrows.

"It's an American term. You behave like one of their politicians, accomplishing absolutely nothing. At 2 p.m. precisely, head back here to Saint Petersburg."

"On the jet, right? Not the train again."

"Yes. The Sukhoi-Gulfstream S-21. Show the pilot this order." She handed him a piece of paper. "He will advise you the moment he leaves Moscow air space. You are to press three buttons in this sequence." The czarina demonstrated on the remote.

"That's all?" He laughed.

"You mess up, and it goes poorly for you. We'll have to destroy the evidence, with a missile or something."

Raspi realized he had no options. He took the remote. "Batteries?"

"Brand new. From Japan."

"And when I return?"

"I'll show you."

She leaned in to kiss him on his lips.

Anastasia moved her kisses down his torso.

"What are you doing?"

"They don't call it the Royal Head Board for nothing."

• • •

It went according to plan. The flight down in the Sukhoi proved effortless. Once landed and deplaned, Raspi headed into Moscow center, witnessing the huge crowds surrounding Vladimir Lenin's mausoleum. Not far from there, he shopped at the GUM department store. Then, back to the airport, and off toward Saint Petersburg.

Ten minutes later the pilot, in Russian, advised over the intercom.

"Now exiting Moscow air space."

Fingers shaking, Raspi entered the three button sequence.

Things immediately went to hell.

• • •

The return flight from Madeira was long and lonely. Chinese Empress Ling An-yee wanted to share it, and the remainder of her life, with Magus Crayle. He was intelligent, kind, virtuous, and well-built, just not overly so.

He also didn't present the challenge any other man would. Crayle wanted no power, no wealth. Just to use his faculties in the best possible way.

She'd become infatuated with his powerful mind early on, but the new Crayle—since his accident—sought only peace, harmony, and stability for all.

He'd want no part, through marriage, as Emperor of China. Rather, she could see him as Chief Advisor to the Empress. To her.

She figured she could woo him away from his wife, if they weren't totally committed to each other. Ling could match sexual prowess with any woman, but there was Hekka's physical beauty. And that butterscotch skin.

She took a moment, glancing at her own flesh. Hmmm. Not butterscotch.

"Ah!" she said aloud.

"Caramel!"

No. She'd just have to wait and see if destiny called her name.

That notion brought a smile.

• • •

Later that day, as she prepared for her birthday party, other thoughts dogged her mind.

When Crayle last visited Hong Kong, he'd located and killed her birth father at the virology lab. He'd pulled down, in spy parlance, the very man who'd help connect his relative, General Li, with her adoptive father and later husband, Chin Yao-wu. The general who, in a younger incarnation, had killed Magus' birth father.

Perhaps things had evened out, then.

That brought her back to her one true love. Mag Crayle.

"You are thinking of him again," Yellow said, walking up from behind and waking her from her reverie.

"I'm obvious, I know."

"I may have the answer. But, to have him as your own, you would have to leave Hong Kong for three weeks. But, look. I've been around you long enough that I know all the issues. More important, I know how you operate."

"You know, Yellow, that I ultimately wish independence for Hong Kong, and full democracy for the mainland. I've reasoned that the extreme political ideology, Communism, did not just imprison our westernmost provinces of the Uighurs, but also those in power. Our leaders could not cobble a system that facilitates social justice while utilizing Capitalism to pay the bills."

"As you said, Communism demonizes Capitalism. To a fanatical extent."

"So many of our own leaders were killed by the mini-nuclear explosion in Beijing's Underground City. Do you think there are any left?"

Their attention abruptly turned to a solid gold, fighting dog statue in the corner of the room. It's eyes glowed red.

Yellow produced a remote control from her purse. She pressed ON.

The dog rotated 180 degrees to reveal an ultra-high-definition flat screen television embedded in its back side. Ling's eyes went wide.

"Look!"

"There's been an explosion!"

Textual overlays indicated that the scene was of Moscow, delivered in real time.

A nuclear mushroom cloud loomed over the city center. A closed caption at the bottom of the screen rendered the Russian journalist's dialog into Chinese.

"My God! She's done it!" Ling caught her breath.

"Who did what?"

"Czarina Romanova has killed her adversaries. She's blown up Russia's main city. That leaves Saint Petersburg as the lone and remaining capitol. Red Square. The Kremlin. Government buildings. Everything up in smoke. All gone."

Yellow affected the Chinese version of the French shrug. She knew quite a bit about Communist remnants. She'd been in touch with them the whole time.

A special chime interrupted further repartee on the future of the empire.

"It's happening!" Yellow exhorted, as she ran toward the long drape exit.

"What? What?"

"It's White … she's giving birth!"

CHAPTER 45

President Stones sat in the Oval Office. At times, he wished he were in Crayle's shoes. Travelling the world. Always a heartbeat away from certain death. Well, maybe not so much.

And sometimes American President Kimbel Stones wondered why his primary work space was designated the Oval Office. Oh, it had the requisite shape all right, but the burdens that tended to enter here pointed to a more descriptive designation. The Oval Orifice.

He'd just hung up his special black phone, having processed and re-processed the contents of a forwarded voice mail. That it had been encrypted on the originator's end, decrypted on the receiver's end, and the process repeated using a secure forwarding app was transparent to the terminal recipient.

Stones heard his friend, chief operative, and sometime strategist for the future direction of Central Intelligence. His messages always provided cause to worry. The master strategist, Mag Crayle, had been principal in the overthrow and transfer of power in France. Done. Check. Prior to that, the same outcome in China. People's Republic to Empire. Done. Check.

The Chicoms had fabricated the weapons of their own destruction. They acquired uranium cake from the occupied country of Tibet. They'd thrown it into the cooker. Turned up the heat. To High. Fissile-wise hot enough, yet small enough to be fabricated inside what appeared to be a normal blimp-shaped rugby ball, with enough space to achieve critical mass. It was likely a little more complex than that, but Stones felt he grasped the basics.

Back to the message as relayed by off-the-books CIA boss, Jack Sommers.

The Crayle voice mail both warmed him and set him to worry.

Portugal.

Stones rubbed his chin. How was Portugal in play? He couldn't just pick up a phone and ask his national defense leader, "Hey, is Portugal in play?" Or his National Security Advisor. He imagined the buzz and kinetic output that would cause at the NSA and CIA. He remembered the Crayle message word for word.

"This message is for Kimbel, Jack. Please see that he gets it. This is bigger than big, so I had to use the unofficial channel between you and me for security reasons. Keep it away from Company ears.

"I'm here in India. A once Portuguese outpost called Goa. On the extended vacation you authorized. I've blundered into a plot with a familiar ring. It seems we have more Illuminé types popping up with the destruction of those we've accomplished elsewhere. I'm tired of playing whack-a-mole with these guys, Kimbel. Really and truly tired.

"I've gained sufficient intel to get in and set up. Jack will have to supply a couple of operatives. It's be a hell of a lot easier if I had the language skills I'll need in Lisbon and Porto. But, I've faked my way to success before, so I'm good.

"I'll keep you up-to-date. Please send any comms for me via Jack. Keep you out of the line of fire. I know you're trying to focus on the next election. Moving into the presidency on your predecessor's suicide determined the near future for you. Now, you can run on accomplishments and shape the campaign.

"I'll try to minimize minor side distractions such as mini-nuke destruction in North Africa and the Iberian Peninsula … you'll want to stay focused." He waited a beat. "Ciao, Kimbel. Crayle out."

Given his own auspicious beginnings at the NSA, Stones was familiar with spies communicating in a distinct, succinct style. That the Crayle message weighed in on the verbose side led him to believe there might be a hidden meaning contained. Still, he couldn't have the pros at Central Intelligence running their code-breaking algorithms on this one. Crayle's directive was crystal clear: Crayle, Sommers, Stones. No more. No less.

Just then, a special coded knock sounded on the door.

"Enter."

Stones shook his head. How to help out a friend?

In through the off-white door walked his chief speech editor. The one he'd lifted from Silas Treadwell's San Ernestino Observer when he'd left.

He sat back, formed a steeple with his fingers, and gave her a most curious look.

Luisa, Portuguese by birth, turned her head to one side, her eyes still fixated on her boss.

"What?"

• • •

Following the Summit, Jack whisked the team from the Hotel Riu, *Compliments of the President,* to a large field. They exited the SUVs into a blinding sun.

What they saw at one end invoked the philosopher, Yogi Berra. "*Déjà vu* all over again." Just as in Australia's Hunter Valley north of Sydney, a large band stand.

Roadies put the finishing touches on the instrument and P.A. connections. The speaker systems blasted out what seemed to be the notable history of Classic Rock.

Plain clothes police escorted the team to a fenced area just shy of the stage. And supplied each of them with air-pressure sensitive ear plugs.

"All right," said Crayle. "Kimbel is making up for past transgressions."

"Such as continually putting our lives in danger."

"Yes. That."

Micmac stepped over to a nearby band groupie. He shouted, "Who's playing?"

"A British group! They're a sacrilegious bunch! Call themselves … get this … The Apostles!"

"Thanks!"

Micmac returned and informed the team. It was the ashen look that took over Crayle's countenance that drew their attention. People responsible for protecting others—notably cops, soldiers, and spies—didn't believe in coincidences. Still, they did exist. Sometimes.

His quandary was, at that moment, resolved.

The mistress of ceremonies stepped up to the microphone.

"And now, without any ado whatsoever, The Apostles!"

The crowd, having gotten a serious alcohol and drug head start, cheered as if she'd said, "The Rolling Stones."

An opaque floor-to-rafters and side-to-side translucent plastic sheet pulled away, revealing the band.

"I'm Matthew on lead guitar. That's Mark on rhythm guitar. Luke on bass. And Jane on the drums."

Crayle nearly passed out. "What …"

Click, click, click, click. Jane's drumsticks counted them into their opening number. Something they called Coincidence. About running into someone you knew on the other side of the globe. Coincidence? Or SOP.

There they were. The Brit black ops team he'd worked with in the Emirates.

"Mag!" Micmac tugged on his arm. "That's them?"

"It is. I need to have Rorschach check Kimbel's sense of humor."

"Spies are supposed to go unnoticed."

"And, if noticed, not remembered."

"Then, there's the hiding in plain sight ploy."

The Apostles finished the song to grand applause. When they'd quieted sufficiently, Matthew spoke again. "Thank you! Madeira rocks!" Hoots and hollers from the crowd. "I've spotted a super musician among you lot." He pointed. "Mick MacKay, ladies and gentlemen. Come on up."

Micmac looked to Crayle.

"Go!"

He gave his friend and colleague a firm push.

"*Go!*"

And so the former SEAL and current American spy did as requested.

For a couple of seconds, he and Matthew traded whispers.

Crayle scanned his team. Hekka, Phoebe, and Alona appeared ready to dance. Lenny just stood there with eyes wide open and eyebrows pushed high.

Jane clicked them in again, and Micmac, now sporting a spare Gibson Les Paul Custom, began a signature opening riff. From the 1960s. Then, a first verse Crayle remembered too well. Words that hit home.

"*There's a man who leads a life of danger.*"

• • •

No sooner had the song ended, than a drizzle began. The band had a tarpaulin overhead and neither risked getting soaked or electrocuted.

On a big screen behind the band, they showed old footage from Woodstock 1969. It was the scene where the rain had just begun to fall.

Crayle turned to his team. They were rocking out to Micmac and the Apostles as if the skies remained sunny.

Back to the screen. As the drizzle evolved into a downpour and Woodstock approached flood proportions, the camera focused in on a young mother and her child.

Crayle couldn't believe his eyes.

On instinct, he turned.

He was tall enough to see past the back of the crowd.

There she was!

Just a much older incarnation.

His own mother!

Right there on Madeira!

She looked at him as he pushed his way through the rocking throng.

But she turned away. And walked at a quick pace toward an outlying building.

He arrived only moments later, following her inside.

Surprise number two.

A man he recognized only too well.

A man in a white lab coat. With a bald pate, and a surrounding berm of pure white hair.

Doctor Rorschach.

• • •

When Crayle awoke, he found himself seated on his mother's lap. Not the little kid who might have done that in his early youth, but a fully grown man.

He jumped up, clutching his head.

"Ahhh!" he cried out.

He stumbled to the corner of the room. Turned. And sat. Elbows resting on his knees. He felt a pinch in his arm.

Doctor Pirmin Rorschach, who lapsed into his Swiss accent whenever he became excited, withdrew the emptied syringe. “Eet vill calm you.”

Almost immediately, the man in the corner began to calm. The terror inside his head began to subside. His breathing slowed to normal.

The doctor reached down, as did his mother, who’d stepped near at the panic of the previous moment.

• • •

His eyes sprung open as he awoke from Rorschach’s chemical panacea.

About to go stark raving mad, he left them both behind, and sloshed through the morass of rain and mud back to his crew.

The Apostles were done, and Micmac was back with Phoebe, Hekka, Lenny, and Alona.

Crayle gathered them up.

In one half hour, they’d returned to the hotel for their luggage, and checked out with an exceptionally generous tip added to Jack’s Black Card. Less than an hour later, they arrived at the airport and boarded the jet.

Next stop, Lisbon.

On the way home.

Sure.

CHAPTER 46

Juan Carlos Mendoza had his first dust ups with Roman Catholicism as a student. He'd been imbued by his Creator with a natural inquisitiveness, which later led him to the Spanish intelligence service. Unfortunately, raising tough questions in school regarding a naturally enigmatic religion did not process well with those in charge.

Nuns, not up to the challenge he presented, would feign outrage, then relegate him to the hallways, assign multitudes of Hail Mary penances, and pray for permission to flagellate the offender.

He became an avid fan of football, not soccer, but the American kind. He'd become an American someday and, to that end, excelled in his English classes. He spoke the language whenever possible. He came to despise his mother religion as anti-intellectual. That led him to a very secret organization. One founded by atheists.

"*Amigo! Linea très! Los Americanos!*" came across the room. He waved off his long time comrade and number two, stepped into his office, and tapped Line 3 on his Smartphone.

He listened.

"*Bom dia!*" came the familiar voice. "Good day!"

Not the American at the CIA, but his own Illuminé compatriot in Sintra, Portugal.

"*Buenos Dias*," he replied. "Good days," he translated, completing the verbal handshake, and switching to English. "I have opened the door. The drilling can proceed from the West border of your country, and ever eastward to Seville. Phase One. Phase Two will transit from that place to the Mediterranean."

"You have a long coast. Where in the Mediterranean?"

"TBD. It depends on a few things. I should have it certain by the time you reach Seville."

"You know I plan to transport the nuclear bombs via the tunnel."

"Yes. To bore an underground passage big enough for ships to pass is a magnificent accomplishment. The German equipment will not falter. We shall meet or exceed our schedule."

"That is crucial. But what of the seismic activity our drilling, however deep, shall insinuate?"

"I have co-opted the premier Spanish seismologist. We're covered."

"Perfect. I travel to Serpa near our eastern border to supervise operations later today."

"And my home town, Seville?"

"In a few days. We should meet to raise a glass of my country's best port. I've been saving a special bottle."

"As we have discussed, there shall be no such meeting for security purposes. And it would be a bottle of Spanish sherry I've been saving."

"Perhaps a virtual toast, then."

"Yes. Virtual. We must stay dark until you are one day out of Seville. At that time, I'll provide intelligence for the remainder of your dig."

"Then, from sea to shining sea. You must choose a site for your future palace."

"It was to be Monte Carlo, but our former Illuminé comrade, Pattie, nuked it. I'm still amazed that we both bedded her, and lived to tell."

"We should form a club of Pattie survivors."

They shared a laugh.

• • •

The Spaniard set down the phone, and considered his grander scheme.

He'd surely given the Portuguese enough reason for his participation. But his sound-muted television said it all. There, on the flat screen, stood the new King of France, Jean-Marc, whose ancestors had been deprived of their rightful succession to the throne. Guaranteed by bloodline.

His own suffered a similar debasement and prohibition from their due. He should've been Prince Juan Carlos, not Deputy Director of the *Centro Nacional de Intelligencia*. The National Intelligence Center, of Spain's southern Andalusia region. Then, King of Spain. That Spain had governed the now Portugal until the year 1139 only underscored that, once he had what he needed—a nuclear bomb—he'd see to the permanent removal of his partner in crime, Martim. At that time, Spain would re-define the country of Portugal back to its original duchy status, and rule the entirety of Iberia. Perhaps from Andalusia. Perhaps from Seville.

Two bombs would do nicely. Three, even better. He'd skip a portion in his drilling so that, even if waters from the Atlantic and Mediterranean entered from either end, there would be no tunnel from sea to sea.

And, utilizing the same Crayle strategy as the Lalumières in France, he'd get the current government to convene in Madrid with one bomb, then take them out with a second. Just like Jean-Marc's father, Sylvain, had done in Marseille and then Paris. Well, almost in Paris. A well-designed Plan B took the French government out in Xian, China. He'd work up his own Plan B, just in case.

• • •

Martim Braganza closed off his end of the conversation with the Spaniard, and tossed his phone into a desk drawer. The drawer was fully lined to prevent any cell tower interaction or recording of conversations in his office.

"You're deep in thought," his wife said as she entered from behind him.

Whenever she did this via a secret entry, his heart jumped.

"Please don't do that! Sneak up on me!"

"Once again, I apologize."

"Just don't do it. Wear a bell or something."

"Yes. I'll have one custom made. In Switzerland. I shall have my own unique sound."

"I'm sorry. Please, take a seat."

She did, facing him. "I want to hear about your chat with the Spaniard. Are we on?"

"We are. We'll finish the drilling from coast to coast in a few days."

"Then, you will pay him?"

"As I've told you, there was a time when Spain lorded over our Portugal and its people. My research indicates that his Spanish ancestors were in power."

"You said they relished their maltreatment of your own forebears."

"When I have my tunnel, I'm afraid he will have to exit."

"Stage left, or stage right?"

"Stage six feet under."

"Hmmm. I've never killed. Perhaps you will allow me the opportunity to become blooded. Résumé fodder for when I become queen."

She was dangerous. He knew that. Perhaps he'd become Iberia's initial widower king.

But, first things first.

• • •

With the Brazil-sexual Flori at the helm, the team's flight from Madeira on the Falcon jet had been peaceful with little turbulence. They'd deposited Micmac, Phoebe, Lenny, and Alona at a premier hotel in Lisbon—to be available as needed.

Crayle and Hekka transferred to a place north of town called Sintra. The magic of the place seemed to invade their senses even before they'd stepped out of the host-provided limousine.

A man, who announced himself only as The Assistant, showed them into the main hall. A light voice greeted them.

"Welcome to Palácio da Pena, Mr. and Mrs. Crayle."

A woman guided them to a period love seat.

"Magus and Hekka."

The Portuguese pointed to himself. "Martim. Future King of Portugal." He nodded toward the woman. "My wife, Beatriz." He turned and waved at a small, translucent window high on the wall behind him.

Music began to play. Not modern or ancient ethnic, rather sounds unexpected.

Crayle recognized it immediately. "*Long Cool Woman In A Black Dress.*"

Martim smiled broadly.

"The Hollies," Hekka casually observed.

Both men threw a surprise glance her way.

Their host turned back to Crayle. "As you can see, I'm 1.7692307 meters. Correct to seven places. Five feet nine inches American."

Few people knew their height out to seven decimal places, Crayle noted. "We should celebrate. How about some Pi? 3.1415927. Seven places."

Hekka viewed the two. "Am I witnessing one of those male what-dogs-call-them contests?"

"The song references the female of the title, Martim."

"It's the only song I could find with my height. As my wife will testify, I am decidedly male."

He showed no such inclination. Martim tossed a special glance at his manservant, who responded in kind. The Hollies song complete, another followed. *Heroes* by David Bowie.

Crayle read the virtual tea leaves. Perhaps Martim swung both ways.

He stood and reached out to Hekka. The mathematician, CIA operative, and master strategist had some moves. She joined in.

The staid Martim recoiled.

"Wait! You … I … oh, hell."

Martim gave in and grabbed his wife's hand. The two couples grooved to the distinctive beat.

Smiles all around.

• • •

Two hours later, they'd finished a delicious repast of ethnic specialties, prepared from scratch by The Assistant. Beatriz whispered in Hekka's ear and she, figuring the two men needed a private confab, agreed to go on a shopping trip to Estoril on the coast. Not far.

When he'd heard the front door close, Martim turned his attention to Crayle.

"I have a special room where we can talk, Senhor Crayle."

"What about Hekka?"

"Oh. I took the liberty. My wife will show her around Sintra. It's Portugal's most romantic place. She'll love it. Then, shopping in Estoril."

Before Crayle could respond, The Assistant approached.

"The room I have for our confidential conversation is isolated, as you would say. But, I'm afraid I'm a bit paranoid." He noticed his guest's reaction. "Not paranoid schizophrenic. Just paranoid." He smiled.

"Just paranoid? Thank goodness."

CHAPTER 47

"Empty your pockets," The Assistant ordered when they arrived at the room. He held out a Sterling silver serving tray after setting glasses of Port wine before them.

Crayle pulled a wallet, his spring loaded metal encased author's notebook, a few keys on a fob, and an eight-inch-long electronics controller. The latter he didn't drop into the tray with the rest.

The man gestured toward him with the tray. "That, too!"

"It's okay," his boss indicated. "A harmless remote control. This American version won't even operate here in Portugal."

Crayle pointed the CIA Universal Remote toward a 100-inch flat panel, and pressed ***TV***. In milliseconds, the device determined the relevant communications protocol, the set's make and model, switched it to ***ON***, and selected the English-language international news channel.

The Portuguese took a minute to process what just occurred. He turned. "Assistant?"

The Assistant grabbed for the device, hitting Crayle with a shoulder as he did.

Crayle shoved him back on his heels with his free, right forearm, clicked ***MODE***, then the number ***2*** with ***ABC*** next to it—for Crayle—then ***1*** and ***ENTER***.

As The Assistant recovered and attacked, Crayle One—his CIA assassin incarnation—blocked the tray wielding arm. He struck a sequence of three nerves, all on the same side of the body, something he'd learned from Ling. Death Touch.

The Assistant collapsed.

Crayle heard a click from behind.

Martim sat behind his desk still, but now with a 10.9 mm Mauser Zig-Zag loaded, cocked, and pointed at him.

Crayle returned ***MODE*** to ***3***. The current incarnation of a spy trying to comprehend what Rorshach's mind manipulations had done to him.

"I'm sorry about Phuket, Mr. Crayle. You probably realized that the staged event was to put you in James Bond mode, but not kill you."

"That was a lot of work to push me in a direction you wanted. There must've been a simpler way. An email, perhaps?"

Martim's paranoia eased off. He decocked the revolver and replaced it in his drawer. He nodded at Crayle.

"So you close off the Strait of Gibraltar with your little scheme. With your bombs. What does that accomplish? Illuminé wants global domination. So, why the Strait?"

"No ships will pass in or out. No supplies. No oil. Nothing that can't be flown."

"But who benefits?" He thought. "Okay. All boat and ship traffic would have to pass through the Suez Canal. Therefore, Egypt benefits. But only for ships that fit."

"So big ship amounts must be re-loaded to Suez Max ships. More money for Egypt."

"Alright. It appears that Egypt's leader is, like you, Illuminé. Go on."

"I don't even know the head of Egypt." He paused for a moment. "Look. Here, it is. America and China ship the most. From America around the African cape to the Suez. Too long. Too expensive."

"So you intend to starve Mediterranean countries?"

"American ships come here. You saw the extensive modifications being made to Lisbon port? By my companies?"

"You'd have to transport, by truck or train, all the way across the Iberian Peninsula. Impossible. You'd have to incorporate Spain into the deal. Your arch enemy."

"If I've learned one thing in all my years, it's that the Spanish leadership in Madrid will always whore out if the price is right."

"I'm thinking that an enriched Portugal is not your end game."

Martim affected a cat-swallowing-canary smile. "Transporting *across* the peninsula, you presumed. How about under it?"

"Oh. I see. I've some relevant history. Perhaps that's why I'm here. A tunnel built by the Aryans. They're very good at tunnels. Underground. Vacuum sealed. A three-hundred-mile per hour railway."

"Like the one you should remember from the Eagle's Nest to Neuschwanstein south of Munich? Like the one you rode from your recent capture in Puerto Madryn, Argentina to Frutillar, Chile?"

"I'll give Illuminé one thing. Its ability to collect data, make it useful, and accessible to all top operatives around the world. Good comms, as we'd say."

"Good comms, and good intel, as you in the spy business would say."

Crayle produced an elongated sigh. "I'm tired of fighting, Mr. Braganza."

He realized he'd completed the sentence in perfect Portuguese. He'd been conversing in the language the entire time.

Rorschach!

He regained his focus. Back to his host.

"Capitulation isn't in you, Mr. Crayle."

"If I press the right button on the remote, I transition back to what is known in select circles as Crayle Two—"

"—allow me to interrupt. The CIA master strategist. One willing to sacrifice thousands of innocent lives during the implementation of your Blackstone Strategy. The one you created, or crafted, for Chin Yao-wu. As aforementioned Crayle Two."

Crayle nodded.

The host led them from the special room back to their previous seats in the living room. Just in time.

"Ah. I heard a door slam outside. Our wives have returned. Please make yourself at home while I consider your offer of Crayle Two … to assist me. I'd have The Assistant show you to your room … but it seems he's dead. I must remember to phone the agency. To have him replaced." He turned and pointed out a hallway. "Twelfth door down on your left. If you need anything, and you haven't killed them all off, my kitchen staff and I'm sure, your beauteous wife, will see to your needs."

The women entered the front door, all smiles and laughter. Hekka walked to her husband and planted a kiss.

"Did we miss anything?"

• • •

Receiving no response, the two women decided to step outside and lounge next to the pool. Beatriz undressed.

A cup of coffee later, the men were back at the private Portuguese version of a Sound and Technology Isolated Facility.

Crayle was, by now, intrigued.

"Digging a tunnel big enough for commercial ships hasn't been done. You'd need multitudes of boring machines going back and forth for months. And you'd need to leave enough at each end to preclude a break through from the tremendous water pressure from the ocean and the sea that would inundate the machines and workers. Once the water's in, all work would cease. Forever."

"I do love your systems insights, Senhor Crayle. All that you've surmised is true, but I got ahead of those problems, most of them, by employing an ally. A German. As you foresaw earlier, an Aryan German."

Crayle's eyes widened. "Of course. Besides tunnels, the Germans have a long reputation for the ad hoc creation of new devices."

"He created for us a boring machine that could handle a ten meter diameter bit. Then, created the bit."

"Hmmm. About 32.5 feet across. You don't send something that heavy and that large via DHL. It might attract attention."

Martim Braganza smiled. "It took two years to dismantle and send from the port in Kiel, Germany. The German and his workers stayed here the entire time, going off each day to reassemble what had arrived."

"The re-integration team didn't draw inquiries from locals?"

"Yes. The fair-skinned, blond-haired men did cause a stir. Short spiked hair with colored tips. Add to that the boisterous manner in which they drank their beer in the off hours."

Crayle recognized the signature look of the Ferals, who'd almost gotten him before. Recently. In Australia. "I imagine at least twenty of them."

"Beers?"

"No. Workers."

"There were only seven. Their leader did belabor the racial superiority thing, especially annoying with me and mine being Portuguese."

"Does this German have a name?"

"You wouldn't know him, but his name was Otto."

Crayle engaged the Portuguese directly. "Otto?"

"A common name in his homeland."

Now, the American spy's eyes shifted to the floor between his feet. The thousand-yard stare. His team's experience with a sequence of Germans of that name had nearly been terminal. They'd not been Illuminé like the bulk of his adversaries, but seemed to have been replicated from a near-perfect example of their ethnicity. Adolph Hitler's dream squad. The Aryan Alliance.

"Senhor Crayle?"

He looked up. "You have to drill the tunnel, end-to-end, and somehow punch open the ends simultaneously. With but one boring machine. You could use a bomb at each end, but the explosion and shock would cave the whole tunnel. You'd have a water channel from the Atlantic to the Mediterranean." He gave it a moment's thought. "Actually … brilliant!"

The Portuguese was visibly upset. Quick, he refilled his glass. "That would have been brilliant if I'd thought of it. Besides …" He regarded a bit. "… I need two bombs for my purpose. To close the Gibraltar Strait."

Crayle concentrated. He had to lose his own genius of an idea to take the intact tunnel notion farther.

"You only need two mini-nuke bombs for your enterprise, but you've obtained three."

Moments of silence passed. The Portuguese was causing him to think.

"The third … it's payment for the drilling equipment. You've given the fanatical Aryan Alliance a nuclear weapon without any concern as to how they'd deploy it!"

"Calm, Senhor Crayle. Otto shared his plans with me. How they'd utilize their single device to conquer their homeland. Not a problem for Iberia, or for the United States."

"I'm inclined to agree with you. From what I know."

With that, he appeared to close off the subject. But, like so many other things, he'd just pushed it to the back burner for a later time.

Then, Martim's phone rang. He examined the caller ID, and answered.

"*Sieg Heil,* Otto." He covered the microphone and whispered to Crayle. "It means *long life.*" A smile, then back to his call. "Ah, that's very good news. We'll be there shortly."

He hung up.

"*Ausgezeichnet!*" He turned to his guest. "Excellent! The machine has been reversed, since it can't be turned around, to a nearby location. I will take you for a ride to the tunnel's end. West end."

"What about Hekka?"

The Portuguese checked an instant message.

"She's with my wife. On another trip. She'll be fine. Beatriz will look after her."

CHAPTER 48

It began for Felipe when he was just a child. In the southern Spanish city called Seville. Even as a young man, he knew his intellect would serve him well in life. Upon learning sufficient English in school, he took to describing himself as a Sevillian. He reasoned to his friends that joking in a foreign language indicated a measure of mastery.

His father would drive into town every few weeks to get his hair cut. He didn't notice at first, but after a couple of years, it became a curiosity that the two of them and the barber were the only ones in the shop.

The adults always spoke of things he didn't comprehend, but that was typical with grownups and he paid little attention. At times, they'd lower their voices to a whisper which had no effect on a mere child. Instead, the boy furtively watched the goings on outside the large window.

He found it frustrating that boys he knew would see him inside, take the opportunity to make faces, or to make obscene gestures. Breaking loose and teaching them a lesson was at the forefront of his mind. Conversely, the young girls who'd gaze at him, nodded, giggled, and ran away. He supposed he would marry one some day, have his own son, and bring him to the same barber. He hadn't been confronted yet with the fact that humans, like his barber, didn't live forever.

When it came time, he decided that barbering was his chosen profession. Conversing about serious adult matters, definitely appealed to him. The barber, old by this time, took him on as an apprentice.

He'd not been aware of his father's role as an illegal arms dealer's money man. Something that the dying man shared just before passing away.

So, that was it. He became both the money man and the conduit when his father and the barber passed, both in the same month.

One of the clients he received from his hair cutting mentor was Juan Carlos Mendoza. The man could be somewhat arrogant and talk down to him, though, without the money, he would be reduced to nothing. There were times he'd restrained his compulsions while using a straight razor.

As he finished removing the last comb from its disinfecting solution, the small brass bell dangling over the front door tinkled.

Speak of the devil. His premier client looked the part of the legendary shaggy dog. Clearly, he'd been busy.

"I don't need lectures, Felipe. I can't go into details, but I'm involved in what the Americans call heavy lifting."

"No problem. I can always assume your work is in Spain's best interest. Can't I?"

"With no exception. My current project will bring untold wealth to our country in need. When I'm through, we may both need to move to Madrid. When I've returned the Spanish monarchy as the ruling element, I'll need a barber I can trust."

He smiled over his shoulder at Felipe, who brought forth a newly sharpened razor. One with a handle in royal purple.

Juan Carlos continued. "The new post would lift you high above your current, lowly station in life."

The barber switched to a less sharp blade.

"Ow!"

The tiniest drop of blood possible appeared. The barber applied a styptic pencil to quell the micro-emission.

"Ow!"

Then, "Now, where was I?"

• • •

With bags from her first shopping trip with Martim Braganza's wife, Beatriz, still in the SUV, Hekka added the just-purchased ones, and turned to the left to address her new friend.

"Let's drop these off at the airport. I suspect Magus and I will be heading home soon, and I don't want to clutter up your fine palace."

Beatriz pressed the intercom button, and so informed the driver.

"You plan to leave when our husbands complete their confab?"

"We do appreciate your hospitality. It's time to get back."

Beatriz changed demeanor.

"That won't be relevant."

"How's that?" Hekka asked beneath squinted eyes.

"Martim advised me before you arrived. We'll be needing your Magus for as long as it takes. Then, I'm afraid, my husband will be finished with him."

Hekka noted that she dragged out the word, finished, a little too much.

In a flash, Beatriz produced a stun gun. One trimmed in feminine pink.

By instinct alone, Hekka reached under her purposefully loose blouse. She popped a snap on the Bowie.

Her now assailant lunged the device for a throat strike.

Something from a college class in self-defense kicked in.

Hekka whipped her left fist upward, and threw an outside-in forearm to block the attack.

Snap! cracked the device as it barely missed.

Yanked from its sheath nestled between her breasts in upside down, jungle configuration, the ten-inch Bowie punched its way under her attacker's bottom rib, punctured the diaphragm, and cleaved both ventricles of the heart in the aftermath.

The eyes of Beatriz glazed over before Hekka gently closed the lids. She left the Bowie in place to stanch the blood flow.

An opaque divider between the driver's compartment and behind precluded both auditory and visual interface between occupants. Only a back seat-actuated intercom permitted instructions, and other sounds, to reach the driver. She reached into a shopping bag and deployed a box of Portuguese feminine hygiene pads to ensure the telltale liquid couldn't drench the floor and ooze forward under the driver's seat.

• • •

At the airport, Hekka stepped aboard the team's jet. In short order, she debriefed pilot Flori.

Behind her, the bedroom door flew open.

Hekka reached for her Bowie.

Gone!

Still embedded in Beatriz!

Not to worry. Micmac stepped out, holding the door with one hand for Phoebe and Alona, while deploying the other to hold Lenny in abeyance until the ladies had passed.

After a hearty sigh, Hekka read them in on the happenings thus far.

Then, a second surprise.

The always Brazil-sexual Flori cleared her throat. They all turned to face her as she related updated orders. She spoke to them in her soft, always Brazil-sexual tone.

"All of you save the sailor will accompany me. To a Spanish town. Seville. I'll fill you in on the way. Micmac stays here, cajoles the SUV driver out there to take him to the palace. To fetch Magus. Uh, Mr. Crayle." She turned to him. "You'll dispatch anyone as necessity requires, and gather up Magus. En route, you'll be secure-texted the specifics of what comes next."

• • •

Micmac crossed the tarmac from Flori's Falcon jet and hopped into the SUV's passenger seat. Before the driver could yell at him to get out, he threw an extended-middle-knuckle punch to the man's windpipe. The man gasped to no avail, and collapsed in his seat.

Since the vehicle was electric with an auto drive feature, Micmac entered codes on his Smartphone to vector a hack via the NSA, and selected the Take Me Home function ubiquitous on all such vehicles.

He had some time as the car headed off to check his messages.

Ah, one from Phoebe.

"Just sayin' Hi."

He responded. "How's the flight?"

"Ho hum."

"Ooh. I can feel that hum from here!"

There was a brief pause while Phoebe laughed. Then, "Been out to sea long, sailor?"

He smiled, and clicked off.

Less than half an hour later, the SUV pulled up to the front door of Martim's palace residence.

Micmac unwrapped a chunk of bubble gum from his pocket and tossed it into his mouth.

Just then, the front door popped open. He noticed one of those special camera-enhanced door bells he'd seen on a TV commercial. He, Mick MacKay, could afford such a device. He just couldn't afford the old palace connected to it.

He stepped into the living room to find his team leader, Crayle, with a gun to his head.

"What a pleasure," said the Portuguese Illuminé leader.

Quick, Micmac jabbed his bubble gum onto the business end of Martim's revolver.

Crayle had filched a pencil from a desk. He rammed the gum down the barrel.

"I need to set an alarm," Micmac said.

Before Martim Braganza could stop him, the former SEAL simultaneously pressed the two stopwatch buttons.

A pair of barbs with trailing wires shot forth at warp speed, and embedded their prongs in the enemy's right forearm.

The severe electrical jolt caused the arm's muscles to contract. His index finger engaged the trigger.

The classic firearm exploded, sending angular shards of metal into his face, neck, and chest. His carotid artery raced with his punctured heart to win Cause Of Death honors.

Crayle and Micmac dragged the expired pair, Martim and The Assistant out to the SUV, and loaded them inside.

"I'm glad our host chose the six seater," Crayle opined. "I'll sit in back with three and keep them from getting bored. Tell 'em Lenny jokes. You sit up front and provide the driver with directions." He gave the name the Portuguese had given as an entry point to the east of their current location.

"Serpa, then."

"And the tunnel."

CHAPTER 49

Magus Crayle and team member Micmac made their way into the depths of the trans-Iberia tunnel. Three hundred feet was a long way to descend, especially navigating the multitude of switchbacks and uneven pathways. And toting four dead bodies.

Crayle pulled a bound book from inside his shirt. "I grabbed a manual off Martim's desk just before we left. It's in German, so I'll translate as I read."

"Go!"

"The German drill apparatus stands forty feet high. The bits, there were two, projected at the front and rear of the device.

"Interesting," Micmac observed. "What's the point?"

"Since turning around at one end of a tunnel to operate in the opposite direction could prove impossible, a bit at each end and the ability to rotate the operators' compartment provides the necessary flexibility. If absolutely necessary, it could turn a little, drill a little, turn a little and drill to afford space for drilling in the opposite direction."

Micmac observed the obvious. "Those Aryans don't miss much."

Crayle continued. "Between the treads, a series of conveyors were embedded into the ground to transport crushed rock away. At both ends of the device, the Germans, with their world-renowned ingenuity, built large combs to move rock into the central channel, and crushers to pulverize it onto the conveyor beneath. But, what to do with the crushed rock?"

"I'll bet there'll be enough to create a whole new country."

"My Portuguese host provided me with more information to take to the grave. About halfway along the tunnel's length, on the surface, there's a dormant volcano. Far below ground sits its giant magma chamber, emptied 11,000 years before. That's where the conveyer system dumped the diggings."

"Anything else?"

"Just a little esoterica. The two bits rotate in opposite directions. One always faces forward and the other in the opposite direction. Their opposite and equal torques cancel each other. The flywheel effect with built-in counter ..." Crayle stopped.

Micmac's eyes began to glaze over.

The former SEAL stood in awe of the gargantuan Aryan boring machine. As an apparent homage, it had been painted Caterpillar yellow.

As the operational type he was, he scoured the upper reaches for the operator's domain.

"Here," Crayle said, pulling at two handles on the machine's near side.

Two vertical rails separated, ascending straight up. An articulated ramp swung out to form a rudimentary elevator platform before them. Crayle stepped aboard. Micmac followed.

Each slid a steadying hand along a rail as the mechanism lifted them skyward. At the top, they stepped into a two-person room, its A/C coming to life. Shortly, the temperature leveled off and the humidity abated.

"By the way. Martim let me read the manual before you arrived. The machine's well automated. I memorized everything on what was supposed to be my last journey anywhere. It's funny how each of these megalomaniacs I encounter feels compelled to show off, thus provding that extra chance I need to escape."

"It's your genius status. They know you'll appreciate their evil genius before they eliminate you as a potential foil."

"Nicely said, Micmac. And bloody accurate."

"Speaking of bloody, wonder what our Apostolic English friends are up to."

Crayle examined his watch. "Probably about to raid Martim's Sintra fortress, and take him down. Hard."

"Hard? No renditioning for intel?"

"None."

"Good idea if he weren't already dead."

"I think we've learned to take these Super Tangos out at our first opportunity. Without the top level, megalomaniacal component of our foes, they don't have the egotistical need to keep things going."

"A dead terrorist is a good terrorist."

"I see what you did there. You equivocated Illuminé to terrorists."

"Well, they scare the be-Jesus out of folks so they'll comply. They shove imperious, atheistic intellect down everyone's throat, then ensure there is no opposition."

Crayle showed his colleague the start-up procedure, then lurched the behemoth machine forward.

"Here we come, Atlantic. May God have mercy, and all else He can muster, on our souls."

"Uh, Mag? When we get to the rock wall at the end, how do we flip this thing around? There's no room for a U-turn."

Crayle pressed a button. The entire inside of the circular operators' structure rotated 180 degrees.

"It has the same number of gears in reverse."

"Leave it to the Germans to cover all bases."

After they'd trundled a few hundred yards, Micmac provided an observation.

"I don't smell burnt fuel."

"It's electric. Green."

"Super green, I'd say."

"No need to vent exhaust fumes topside."

"Less of a chance for this whole, crazy operation to be discovered."

Crayle pressed another button. The giant circular drill bit ahead began to turn.

Slowly at first, then picking up speed.

The machine itself also accelerated. Faster and faster. Louder and louder. Punching the controls for speed or braking had no effect.

Crayle's voice penetrated the din.

"*This isn't good!*"

The gargantuan machine raced at about fifty miles per hour toward the solid wall ahead.

The tunnel's end.

CHAPTER 50

One hundred feet.

Fifty feet.

Ten …

• • •

The water incursions began in spurts.

The drill bore on.

Heavy streams exploded through.

"Crap!" Micmac yelled at the percussive sounds of the water bursts.

"Hang on!" Crayle returned. At first glance, he'd wondered why the Germans chose racing seats for a drilling device.

As quickly as possible, the men buckled into the six-point racing harnesses.

The pressure of several million gallons of sea water overwhelmed the remaining wall.

The wall, fending off the entire Atlantic Ocean, gave way.

• • •

The giant drill machine would've turned into the world's largest cork … if it could float.

The Atlantic blew into the tunnel at warp speed. At first, the squeezed down venturi effect accelerated the flow.

The machine's occupants had gone into washing machine mode, unable to thank God just yet that the operators' cabin was solid. And waterproof.

Waterproof was good.

Drastically limited air supply, not so much.

"Any last words, Micmac?"

"Just love to Phoebe and the kid. I want them to be proud of my memory."

"There's good news!" Crayle hollered as the machine tumbled end over end.

"Good news works here!"

"President Stones … he'll get us into Arlington!"

• • •

Having the treads spinning at full speed in opposite directions was an additional touch added by their remote assailants, who'd garnered total control. As a giant wheel hit the bottom, top, or sides of the tunnel, that effect spun them hard sideways.

The human brain can only take so much.

The two men, in excellent physical shape, fast approached their limit.

Then, it happened.

Crayle and Micmac's ride blew past a side tunnel.

The one leading to the magma chamber.

The onrushing Atlantic seized the opportunity.

A significant portion of volume and force siphoned away.

"That helps!"

"The O2 gauge is heading for the red, Micmac!"

"The banging around from the spinning drills and treads makes us use more oxygen."

"I wish to hell they'd stop so we could level out."

No sooner were the words spoken than the drill spin ceased. The tracks next.

• • •

Above ground at the Seville barber shop, four sidearms puffed whiffs of smoke.

Hekka, Phoebe, Alona, and Lenny stood shoulder to shoulder.

The Barber of Seville and his intelligence officer partner in crime looked like the wrong end of a Saint Valentine's Day massacre.

They'd stepped in with weapons pointed at two mouths agape. They fired, each running their clips all the way to empty.

The first rounds, Hekka and Phoebe's, struck the barber. Their impact caused him to draw the razor hard across the Spaniard's throat.

Blood spurted from arteries.

It flowed from veins.

People on the sidewalk outside observed in horror.

It was over in seconds.

Hekka walked to the front door. She flipped the sign from *Abierto* to *Cerrado*. From Open to Closed. Then, pulled down the shade. Phoebe took care of the other windows.

It was Lenny who found the Bluetooth keyboard in a drawer. Not having a display to work from, "Oh, hell," he allowed, and pressed CTL-ALT-DEL. He waited for five seconds, then CTL-ALT-DEL again.

"Yeah!" he exclaimed, glancing over at Alona. "Shut the blanker down!" He hadn't noticed a barber mirror not visible from the street as its latent computer screen disappeared. "That shuts these bad guys down."

With her heart rate de-escalating back towards normal, Phoebe mused, "Wonder what the boys are doing?"

"Yeah," Lenny responded. "They missed all the action."

Unbeknownst to the four, he'd terminated the electronic mayhem Crayle and Micmac experienced with the drilling machine.

• • •

The result of the barber shop activity normalized the situation below. The drill machine still pushed along at a high rate of speed, now remained upright, having the bulk of its weight—its center of gravity—below midpoint.

A snorkel device on the machine provided air to the engine and cabin on an as-available basis. Micmac noticed.

"Without the tunnel being full of water, it's grabbing air!"

Crayle glanced at the control panel. "The O2 is picking up! We're not going to suffocate!"

"Gotta love those Germans."

"Not sure about the Aryan Alliance."

"Especially all the ones named Otto."

"I still recall in detail the chambers beneath that Disney castle in southern Bavaria."

"Neuschwanstein."

"Yeah. By the way, how is it, Mag, that you know German?"

• • •

Perched atop the gigantic machine, the operators' cabin filled with oxygen-rich air. Combined with the reduced water flow, it continued upright as it now cruised ever eastward.

The men unbuckled their safety restraints. For the first time in a while, they relaxed.

Far behind, the waters of the Atlantic finally filled the magma chamber. The side tunnel ceased to fulfill its impromptu role as a relief valve.

The pressure of all seawater above the West tunnel entrance—all over the globe—pushed down. Once again, the full force and power rushed through.

Miles East, Micmac lofted his hand, presenting his new watch. "New idea from me to S & T. They turned it into a watch good to 300 meters with a special feature."

"What, it tells time?"

"More than that. It can send out an ELF beacon. In case we need rescue and exfil."

"For Extra Low Frequency transmission to work, we'd need to be immersed—"

Just then, the renewed water force hit them. With a particular vengeance.

The nature of the hydrodynamics somehow kept the machine upright.

That was the good news.

As the men scrambled to re-link and buckle up, Crayle yelled, "It's propelling us toward the East tunnel wall! Just ahead!"

Grasping a shoulder strap, he reached one of the controls … and pressed.

"You started the drill! What the—"

The flow slammed them against the tunnel's East wall. The drill hesitated, then began to grind.

Shortly, it bored through.

In came the Mediterranean.

The Clash of Titans. Atlantic versus Mediterranean.

Miraculously, the waters neutralized their opposing forces.

About sixty miles South, this ocean and this sea melded in harmony, just West of the Strait of Gibraltar, for millennia.

The drilling machine settled just beyond the tunnel's East opening. On a narrow shelf.

Crayle breathed a sigh. He glanced over at the former SEAL.

"Now, about that watch …"

• • •

A sudden surge due to water oscillation in the tunnel shoved their drilling machine about ten feet sideways. Toward the edge.

"Oh! Micmac!" Crayle caught his breath. "You want to step outside, and send that ELF?"

"Why, sure. I'll hyperventilate, and get 'er done."

He started toward the door. "It's gonna get wet in here."

"I'll follow you out. We're not too far down. I'll follow you to the surface."

"Make sure to breathe out as you ascend. Slowly."

Though a bit battered by the day's events, the two men, both in excellent physical shape, feathered the door far enough open to escape.

• • •

Crayle bobbed up first, gasping for air. He saw the coast of Spain a hundred yards or so distant.

He scanned. What he didn't see was his teammate, Micmac. A few minutes passed. Worry set in. But, the man had been a Navy SEAL.

Up popped a head. Twenty feet away. It spoke.

"Saw something on the shelf."

Hands in the air in exasperation, Crayle responded. "This is no time to gawk."

"I *saw* one of 'em."

"One of what?"

"The bombs."

"You're shitting me."

"I won't call up the Navy response: 'I wouldn't shit an old turd like you.' I'll save that for another time."

"What about the nuke?"

"They had the FRONT TOWARD ENEMY wrong, from our perspective, facing the explosive part sorta sideways. Toward the Strait. I flipped it." He produced a wide smile.

"So the force of a detonation will be directed up. Softened by the water."

More smile.

"Right where we are."

Micmac's smile faded. "Well, I'm outta here. You might want to follow me." He started away.

Crayle pointed. "Land's that way."

"I'll go find the second one … on the other side of the Strait."

"How the hell far can a SEAL swim?"

"As far as it takes!"

As if on cue, the exfil chopper homed in on them. After a side trip to the Africa side of the Gibraltar Strait, and a Micmac free dive to reverse the second bomb, their ride transported them to a port just outside the British enclave.

The gang waited there.

The minute they landed and hopped out the door, a wild cheer arose.

"Hurry up!" Lenny yelled as he waved them onward. "I have the next evolution all set to go! You can rest later!"

Crayle and Micmac stopped in their tracks. Facing each other, they initiated Rock-Paper-Scissors … to see who'd get the honor of killing Lenny.

CHAPTER 51

It was a monumental day. The Crayle spy team, augmented by some notable additions, gathered in La Linea de la Concepción. Not too far from the mouth of the new river in Spain they'd created, it was adjacent to the famous British outpost, the Rock of Gibraltar.

The American president was there along with his political mainstays, Susanna and Luisa. Jack Sommers, who'd just finished out his term as interim Director of Central Intelligence. And off-the-books pilots, Marli and Flori.

There would be, the president told them all, a race. A boat race.

The vessels were pre-assigned. A small shuttle transported Micmac and Phoebe to a beautiful Canova schooner manufactured by Baltic Yachts.

"We thought you'd want a sailboat, having been a sailor and all."

Micmac knew about this superyacht. Sail plus diesel plus electric. It possessed hybrid capability and could run up to nine hours in silent mode. And, at 142 feet, just about perfect for the waters to be navigated. But then he glanced around at their competitor's equipment. It was the 262 foot Artefact by NOBISKRUG of Germany. "I'm supposed to beat them," he swept his arm, "in this?"

Phoebe tried to save the day. "Maybe it has a motor."

"Sailboats have piss-ant motors. Some have none at all."

"Start it up."

He did. The motor roared to life with a deep, throaty growl.

Micmac jumped back. Then, he noticed the two throttle levers on the dashboard.

"Whoa! Twin racing engines on a sailboat!" He beamed, and waved. "Thanks, Lenny!"

Lenny waved back. He held up an object. "My starter gun."

Alona added. "His actual starter gun was the one he was born with."

All laughed.

With Race Control Lenny and Race Judge Alona leading the way, the five teams motored at low speed to the starting line just East of the Gibraltar Strait. It had been no small feat, in preparation for the race, to waylay normal traffic in and out of the waterway. Beaucoup ships passed through on a normal day. But one of the racers did have a degree of special influence.

Kimbel Stones, the American president, and Jack Sommers, DCI pro-tem, brought their boat to a halt at what Jack claimed to be the right spot.

"You sure this is it, Jack? You're the navigator."

"As far as I can tell, Kimbel. But it's an estimate. A government estimate."

"You mean some sort of Wild Ass Guess? A WAG?"

"A SWAG, Sir. A Scientific Wild Ass Guess."

The president frowned. "So, what does it take? I tell your team to address me by my given name, and to avoid calling me *Sir*. And you do it, anyway."

"Sorry, Sssss …" Jack didn't suppress the laugh.

Drawing up on their port side, Marli and Susanna proffered salutes with Jack's ex-wife, Marli, minimizing hers to the expletive-encompassing middle finger. Of her right hand.

Jack turned to Stones. "She still loves me."

The Brazilian team of Flori and Luisa arrived on the starboard side. Though the ladies were American citizens now, they couldn't resist sporting the yellow, green, and blue colors of their native land.

"Bom dia!" they shouted with big smiles and full hand salutes.

Outboard of Marli's boat sat Micmac and Phoebe, the gadget man at the helm. It freed up the on-loan FBI Agent to draw her famous .45 caliber Glock 30 if anything untoward transpired.

Last, far to starboard, Mag and Hekka Crayle motored up to the imaginary line.

While all set their high-powered motors to idle and transmissions to neutral, the diminutive man to their right and just ahead, pointed toward them, and pulled a bullhorn to his lips.

"Peoples of the world," Lenny yelled. "We are gathered here today for the monumental race of our time."

He could hear the applause from both shores with the aggregate of onlookers estimated at twenty thousand.

Alona pulled the bullhorn away long enough to shout, "Don't applaud! It only eggs him on!"

A scowling Lenny reacquired control of the device. "As I said, we are … oh … I already said that."

He waited.

No applause.

"Whine."

No sympathy, either.

Undaunted, he continued.

"Here between the legendary Pillars of Hercules—you've heard about them on TV. Named after the famous guy who invented *My Pillars*!"

Lenny glanced at his team members. They'd lapsed into a collective version of an eye roll—groan combination.

Then, to Jack, and the president.

Stones tried his best to dead pan, but Lenny's lame joke won out. He cracked a smile, then bent over, and let go.

The team followed the president's reaction in succession and, since all had microphones in their helmets, triggered the crowds at their respective Pillars into a cacophony of laughter and heavy applause.

Lenny swept his free arm around as if to say, "See!"

Alona snatched the bullhorn from her distracted husband. "He'll just go on until the boats run out of fuel." She shook her head in his direction. "Ladies and gentlemen. Start your engines!" She thought. "Or, keep them going." She turned. "What's next?"

She brushed his hand aside as he reached for the bullhorn.

He sidled up next to her. Cheek to cheek, they did it together.

"On you mark! Get set! *GO!!!*"

Just then, the mini-nuclear bombs Micmac had repositioned played into the scene. Two underwater explosions sent columns of water skyward on each side of the Strait. Hundreds of feet in the air. The water-muffled sound was still loud enough that all rushed to cover their ears.

At that moment on nearby Gibraltar lights flashed and sirens sounded, the response to an imagined attack.

It was all the signal the teams needed.

Two of the boats leaped forward.

The Crayles and the MacKays.

Then, the rest.

Lenny watched in horror as they sped past.

"Hey!"

He held up his pistol.

"I haven't—"

Too late.

His face turned grim.

Then, "Oh, well."

In frustration, he tried the pistol again.

Nothing.

There he stood, cursing the starter gun as he repeated successive vain attempts to provide the official signal.

Alona'd had enough. "C'mon, Lenny! Deep six the son of a bitch! Get us outta here, and don't stop 'til we see the lights of Casablanca!"

He tossed the offending device overboard, and headed them away. He'd morph to his second role, following the racers as a chase boat, just in case.

Snapped into gear with engines revving high, the boats tore westward across the placid boundary of the Mediterranean Sea. In just minutes, they crossed into the Atlantic Ocean and began to take flight as the waves picked up.

They each throttled back. A little.

This was pure fun and excitement.

The perfect relief for what had been truly trying times, and voluminous danger.

Lenny seized the moment for his second act. But what he saw on the North shore kept him silent.

British, Spanish, Portuguese, French, and Italians smiling and laughing and giving high fives.

He spun around toward the South.

Moroccans, Tunisians, Algerians, Libyans, and even a crowd from Egypt. The same. Laughter. High fives.

His gaze was drawn West.

There were Hekka and Mag up ahead. In the lead.

"Magus Crayle," he muttered.

The Magic Man.

CHAPTER 52

The racing yachts crossed the finish line just outside Morocco's Casablanca harbor. The Crayle boat inched out the MacKay boat for first place.

No sooner had the winning teammates performed the requisite high five than they heard Phoebe over their intercom earpieces.

"Second place? In a boat race? Gotta check those Navy credentials, husband."

"I'll show you my credentials, again, later tonight," he teased back.

As for the Lipshitzes? The others would hear Lenny brag later. "Hey! Third place! A podium finish!"

"You were third of three, hot shot," Phoebe reminded him.

"Still third! The beautiful Moroccan girls will be impressed so I can gather them up into my har—"

Alona interrupted the thought. "You better not say harem, short stuff. I still remember my wedding vow clearly. *'Til death us do part.* Hmmm?"

Lenny clammed up. Without whining. For a change.

It was about two hours shy of sunset and the temperature had cooled to 58 degrees Fahrenheit. Typical for the latter part of December on the Moroccan coast.

A personal guide replete in Berber attire, looking like a ringer for Jack Sommers, whisked the three couples to a well-attended outdoor presentation of trophies, presided over by none other than Kimbel Stones, President of the United States. His presence came as no surprise, though. It was hard not to notice Air Force One flying overhead as they'd closed in on the finish of their race.

• • •

They arrived shortly at a place that looked familiar. The light colored exterior walls plus the arched entrance and heavy wooden door meant something. And then, the neon sign.

Rick's Café Américain.

They were tired, but not too tired to smile. Which they did.

A guide hustled them in via the heavy wooden door and ornate arched frame through the café with its lights dimmed, after hours feel. About all they noticed as they hustled through were the interior archways, the many tables for four, and the lights. Wall lights, hanging lights, and table lamps. The potential for actually seeing anything was there in force.

Like any still-alive spy, Crayle did his best to scan the surroundings for current or potential threats. As his eyes adjusted, their guide led them into the office.

A barely visible trio of light-colored sofas filled approximately two-thirds of the room. They'd been made out into sleepers, one per couple.

In short order, all team members were in bed and fast asleep. The day had, indeed, been long.

• • •

When he awoke, Crayle reached over for Hekka. A natural eyes-still-closed move. His hand padded around. Nothing.

His eyes popped open. Then, he surmised, 'she's in the bathroom.'

No.

He could see that the door was ajar, and the light off.

As he glanced about, he noticed the other sofa beds were empty as well.

Of course. Daylight bled around the closed drapes, and his team, considerate to a fault, had dressed and stepped into the café for breakfast.

He'd just tossed off the covers when he realized he was undressed. A quick peek revealed that, at least, they'd left him with his Calvin Klein briefs. Black like everything else he wore.

No.

They were CK, all right, but charcoal in color.

Hekka must've provided him charcoal-hued fresh underwear. Still, creepy.

But, where were the outer clothes he'd worn the previous day?

A black rack stood next to the bed a few feet away, bearing a full suite of clothes. In his sizes.

He dressed, noting the colors were a bit drab. A medium gray suit over a light gray dress shirt.

He stopped. His eyes panned the room.

Good God!

Every bit of it were shades of gray or flat white.

He got it.

The eponymous movie, Casablanca, had been presented in black and white, or more accurately, shades of gray.

It was as if he were in the film. And the shades of gray euphemistically mapped into his profession. Espionage.

The smile came readily to his lips. Stones? Sommers? Team members? Some or all?

By instinct, he reached under the pillow, retrieving his SIG-Sauer .40 caliber along with its shoulder holster.

The jacket had been altered to preclude a telltale pistol bulge. The smile remained. As a spy, you either pay attention to detail, or you pay attention to your funeral.

Dressed and dapper, he wiped the smile off his face and stepped out the door.

He laughed. So this was Kimbel Stones idea of getting the team to relax.

Now well lit, the entire café presented itself in shades of gray.

Welcome to *Rick's Café Américain*.

Casablanca.

• • •

Crayle took a moment in the office doorway to observe. Before him was arrayed what Hollywood would term extras. Just like the movie.

But how could it be, being an amnesiac with memories serially restored, that the image before him was so vivid?

His smile disappeared.

Rorschach!

The Madeira Session!

The CIA mind doctor had not only insinuated fluency in Portuguese—albeit the Brazilian dialect—but had found reason to play. He'd inserted a classic movie, as well. But, Crayle didn't recall the doctor having that manner of sense of humor. Never one for frivolity.

What was coming next?

He needed to find the others. His team.

As soon as that thought fully processed, he spotted Hekka.

She sat at a table, looking like a very passable stand-in for the Ingrid Bergman character, Ilsa Lund.

He suddenly realized her uniquely beautiful butterscotch skin coloration had been turned, like everything else, to a shade of gray. A pale shade.

He glanced down at his hands. Gray. How hadn't he noticed?

He stepped over and took a chair opposite his wife. He clasped her hand in his.

"Is this Casablanca, or is it the Twilight Zone?"

"Relax, darling. Remember our time in Paris."

He started to nod. But did she speak of their time in the City of Light, *La Ville-Lalumière*, or in character as Rick Blaine and Ilsa Lund from the movie?

As his mind began to swirl, it was interrupted.

Hekka. She'd turned to one side, toward the piano.

"Play it once, Sam."

She hummed a few bars.

He played the intro on the keyboard.

Crayle affected a look that appeared almost desperate. "Sam, I told you never to play …"

"Sing it, Sam," she implored.

Sam, looking for the world like Lenny's Alona in drag, returned, "For the lady."

Alona attended to the keyboard. And began to sing.

"*You must remember this. A kiss is just a kiss. A sigh is just a sigh.*"

Alona paused.

Magus Crayle, a man of proven strength and durability, began to turn to mush.

Emotions were far from a spy's best friend. But, there they were.

Still holding Hekka's hand, he stood.

She followed suit.

They stepped around the table, closing the distance.

The embrace.

The kiss.

Alona, at the piano and feeling the romance, smiled.

"*The fundamental things apply. As time goes by.*"

• • •

Across the room, there was Lenny. His abbreviated height, fit well into his role as Signor Ugarte as originally played by Peter Lorre. His character had apparently killed a pair of Nazi couriers to obtain two letters of transit, necessary for exit from Casablanca. Next to him, and man-handling him with apparent pleasure, stood Phoebe, replete in gendarme attire as Captain Louis Renault, Prefect of Police, and arresting officer.

Lenny did his best. But signature outcries of "Jeez Louise!" and "Whine!" seemed a bit unauthentic with regard to the film.

As the annoyed gendarme extras carted him away, the Viktor Lazlo character arrived. Looking a great deal like Micmac, he suggested they retire to the office to discuss certain documents. Before they got far, Phoebe intercepted them.

"Be careful of these two," she said, nodding at Micmac and Hekka. "They could be trouble."

Crayle considered the former SEAL and his own ten-inch-Bowie wielding wife.

Indeed.

A surprise to anyone who hadn't memorized the movie, Phoebe picked up the volume.

"Everyone is to leave here immediately," Phoebe ordered. "This café is closed until further notice! Clear the room at once!"

Crayle found his plaintive voice. "How can you close me up? On what grounds?"

Phoebe's Captain Louis Renault rendition responded. "I'm shocked. Shocked to find that gambling is going on in here."

At that moment, Alona stepped into the group. "Your winnings, sir." She handed Phoebe a handful of Moroccan Dirhams. She left them with, "I gotta go find Lenny. He probably needs a lawyer by now." She headed for the front door.

"Everybody out at once," Phoebe commanded.

Everyone left.

• • •

With the memories of the movie set clone, *Rick's Café Américain*, and their quasi-lame performances in the rear view, a private coach transported them to their hotel. Jack, seated to the right of the driver, provided a running commentary.

"As we leave the harbor area, to the side over there is the famous Hassan II Mosque. It is positioned 2.2 miles from our destination, your hotel. Over that way," he pointed, "is the Ancient Medina, a mile from your lodging, for traditional shopping. And there, 5.8 miles away from your temporary residence, is the Morocco Mall. Ladies, and I'm not being sexist, it's a place you'll want on your itinerary."

The rumblings from the posh seats didn't bother him. They told him that at least the three women were listening.

"And there is United Nations Square, 2,150 feet from city center. Nearby, your abode for the next few days. And nearby, ladies and gentlemen, I present Hôtel and Spa, *Le Doge*, a *Relais et Château* property. I chose it for its opulence, and as a left-handed tribute to our French friend and ally, Jean-Marc Lalumière, better known these days as King Louis XX."

Crayle spoke up. "When we're finished with this post race R & R, what are the arrangements for exfil … I mean, transport back home. We've all been missing our kids now for way too long."

"I understand, believe me. The spy business isn't much of an environment for children to grow up in."

"Let me remind you, Jack, that the business, as you call it, is responsible for the untimely, simultaneous delivery of three aforementioned babies due to the also simultaneous detonation of three mini-nuclear devices in the vicinity, which initiated three very pregnant operatives going into labor."

"I didn't mean it that way. I … I meant it some other way."

"You're becoming more and more of a politician."

"Okay, okay. I'm sorry as hell. But look. That op saved the centerstone of Australia. Ayers Rock. The Ulurú. You took down the top Illuminé leader of the region."

"And, with this op, one more. When does it end, Jack?"

"Oh, look. We're here. C'mon now. Off and on. We'll get you checked in and I, the noble Jack Sommers, will see that your rooms and all expenses are covered. It will be on the Black Card in the name of Neil Patrick Wohlford, my predecessor as head of the Strategic Solutions Office."

"Yeah, the Illuminé mole Pattie offed in his home town. Did you ever reckon, Jack, that you two would meet up after death?"

"Me and Pattie? No. I'm not going to the same … hey!"

"It's called Eternal Hell, Jack. Now, about our exfil."

"After two or three days, your choice, we'll shuttle you to the private jet aspect of Mohammed V International Airport. Less than an hour from here. Now let's get you inside. And Magus, I need a word with you. Something from the president."

"Congratulations, I hope. I'm done with ops."

"Something like that."

• • •

Fifty minutes later found Crayle and Phoebe and Micmac and Hekka at the Mohammed V International Airport.

In character, Mr. and Mrs. Lazlo, as represented by Micmac and Hekka, replete with Letters of Transit to America, prepared to board the plane to their refueling stop, Lisbon. A drizzle began to fall.

Crayle could think of no one better than himself to have Hekka's safety on the front burner than his retired SEAL, UDT, and weapons specialist teammate and consummate friend, Micmac.

He stepped close to her.

Their eyes met. "You'll just be stopping in Lisbon to refuel. We've already done some time there."

"It's quite the place. First it was Estoril. Then, Sintra."

Micmac intervened. "Hey. That's my wife there. And we've got a plane to catch."

Crayle tossed a smile his way. "We have history. That's all." He took a second. "And this is the love of my life … forever."

They kissed. Deep.

And kissed again.

When their lips parted a final time, he noticed that the dampness in her eyes matched his.

"I've got a little thing to do here before I leave. Not to worry. Phoebe'll watch out for me. I'll see you soon, *shweet hot*."

Hekka recognized the Humphrey Bogart rendition of *sweetheart*.

She stepped back. "And I you."

"Yes, you will. And until that precious moment … here's lookin' at you, kid."

The moment proved as precious as it'd been in the movie.

Shortly, the fake Lazlos were aboard and the plane taxied to the runway. Five minutes later, there it went. Off into the foggy night headed for Lisbon.

Crayle turned to Phoebe, and offered her his arm.

She latched on as they walked away. He smiled as he thought of a better future. "Y'know, Phoebe. This could be the beginning of a beautiful friendship."

CHAPTER 53

It was the next day in Casablanca. Crayle and Phoebe had been hustled off to a meeting set up by President Stones. Or so Jack had informed him the night before. No big deal, Jack had said. Crayle thought of George Orwell and how, in 1984, the reality of something was the exact opposite of how it presented itself. The Ministry of Peace was actually The Ministry of War. No big deal?

Before running off to join the president plus Susanna and Luisa on Air Force One, Jack provided Crayle with a briefcase and materials for a hyper special meeting. He'd just perused them, and shook his head. It was Operation Blue Sky the president had mentioned previously. No big deal?

Still, he was ready for the day and whatever it portended, knowing at its end, he'd be headed home.

The building they'd entered appeared austere enough. A single story of gray cement with one door and no windows. Inside, a Sound and Technology Isolated Facility, or STIF, afforded maximum privacy for all that would be spoken. On the floor lay a map of the Middle East such that each attendee's chair sat on his own capitol.

All ceremonial daggers of the Muslims involved had been retained outside by a Phoebe-supervised team of guards. A serious inspection of the men ensured no bombs and other weapons passed inside.

Magus Crayle, advertised as the facilitator for the meeting, opened the session.

The meeting exhibited a notable religious tenor.

"Gentlemen. My name is Crayle … Magus Crayle. As you are aware, I am the present DCI of America's CIA. I need you to get comfortable. You may order any drinks from the tablet computers on each desk."

"I'll have the shot of Smirnoff." The Jewish chief cleric pecked on his iPad.

"The blasphemy begins," said the Iranian. "There can be no alcohol. Our religion forbids it." He swept a hand at all but the Israeli.

"I'll have the same as him," said the Iraqi. "We are here to bridge gaps, not reinforce them."

"Then we should all have a shot of vodka and an orange juice."

"So shall it be," Crayle said.

They all ordered, and received delivery shortly.

When his drinks arrived, the Israeli ceremoniously dumped his shot into the juice, and lifted his glass. He placed the coaster on top. With a firm grip, he gave his impromptu mimosa a few shakes.

The Muslims in attendance recognized the non-verbal affront ensemble.

The Israeli took a long sip, ending with an "Ahhh!"

It was good that the daggers had been retained outside, although those darting from the eyes left no doubt as to the ire felt.

"Infidel," the Iranian cried out.

The rest either repeated the label, or nodded concurrence.

Crayle jumped back into his role as facilitator. Back to topic.

"So Jews, like Christians, believe in God."

"There is but one God. Allah," said the Syrian.

Crayle glanced over at him. "Please translate Allah to English."

"Why, The God. Of course."

"Then all three religions acknowledge a belief in one god. The creator of everything."

Blank stares.

"Logic says, gentlemen, that everyone's one god is the same god. Further, it means that all three religions point to that same one god, and exist solely for the purpose of pointing individuals in the right direction. It also implies that no one religion is better than the others and, finally, true believers in any of these religions cannot disrespectfully be referred to as non-believers. Otherwise known as infidels."

The line of logic, however correct, failed to work for the Muslims in the room. Declaring opponents as infidels had become a standard component of their political tool kit. "It also means that the One God created the three religions in the first place. Would any of you choose to find fault with what He decided on this issue?" Not one of the participants chose to take on the One God's wisdom.

Crayle continued.

"Each one of those religions should be able to guide us to the proper path. It also means, sadly, that priests, rabbis, and imams, who do other than put believers on the prescribed path … will finish, not in Paradise or Heaven, but in Eternal Hell. Everlasting Eternal Hell."

The silence told him he was getting through.

"Who here believes that the One God, who created an entire universe, who on this planet created life in the form of 1,169,078 species of plants and animals as of 2011, who created religions to show us the way, is weak? Is incompetent? Or requires the assistance of any human being?"

No hands.

"So, if he shows us the way and we don't follow, does he need any human to punish the wrong doer? Short answer, no. When that individual's time on Earth is done, then He determines what is next for that one. If we interfere here on Earth before that God-determined time, He will not be kind."

Crayle could tell they were getting impatient.

"Why do you tell us these things?"

"If we threw all three religions in a blender, we'd end up with one that does everything. It would be the ultimate One God religion."

"He wants us to place the Quran, the Holy Bible, and the Torah into a blender," said the Saudi.

All enjoyed a good, much needed laugh.

"Into the blender? Only the ideas," Crayle said.

"If we become all of one religion … "

"We can no longer fight each other."

"We can't kill each other."

Crayle picked it up from there.

"I know, gentlemen, that would put a lot of people out of work. Religious terrorism would be chasing its tail."

Eyes opened wide. Heads nodded.

"There's more. Rabbi Kushner's country has two labels. Israel, and the Holy Land. What if it became just the Holy Land. Or better. What if the entire Middle East became the Holy Land. You can't separate people by religions if there is only one."

"This is much to consume. And we, upon your orders, have fasted for two days. You promised us a feast. We will work better on a full stomach."

"I did, and you will." Crayle rang a little bell, and chefs trouped in through the vault door.

The smells of hot food quickly filled the room.

"This is an outrage, Crayle!"

"You know we can't eat this!"

They all turned. Crayle was gone. The chefs were gone.

By now, their olfactory senses competed mightily with their religious beliefs.

"I will not eat bacon," huffed the Iraqi over crossed arms,

"Nor I," said the Iranian.

"It is dirty."

"Filthy."

They sat.

They waited.

The Syrian reached to the Iraqi's plate to acquire the controversial food items.

In an instant, the Iraqi smacked the back of his neighbor's hand.

The bacon strips fell back onto the plate.

Before genuine fisticuffs could break out, they were interrupted.

"I shall sacrifice for the good of all," the Israeli announced. He took a piece, and bit off a chunk.

"See," the Iranian barked. "He's eaten the meat of the pig. It is a sign from Allah. Israelis must be destroyed!"

Unphased, the rabbi continued with his repast.

"And now that I … Oh! Oh!" He scanned the room. "This is God's work," he said as he gobbled down the remainder. "Oh! It's proof of God!"

While they all held very low opinions of swine and all they did, the rest dug in, becoming the human version of a drift of pigs at feeding time.

"Oh!"

"*Oh!*"

"You are correct! God's work!"

The Iranian next proved that human beings can rationalize anything.

"Clearly, there was an error in translation of the scriptures."

When the Israeli finally looked up from his empty plate, he noticed Crayle standing behind the others.

"Look," said the rabbi in amazement. "It has disappeared. Another miracle."

That one got them all.

The rest broke into uproarious laughter. Guffaws and all.

Then the feasting pigs turned into weasels.

"You tricked us! It was bacon fabricated of turkey! We … we … we are still clean!"

"Yes! Yes!" the others chimed.

Crayle shook his head. "How can I say this?" He stroked his chin. "You've all partaken of the forbidden fruit." He peered into the once filled-to-overflowing serving dish. He rang the bell once more.

The chefs trouped in and placed an ice cream sundae in front of each man.

"This will clean your soiled palettes."

They all dug in, but one.

"Oh!" they chorused when they tasted the bacon-infused ice cream. "*Oh!*"

"I refuse," the Iranian said.

The Iraqi sitting next to him reached over and slid the new surplus sundae next to his own.

"Oh!"

"Oh!"

The voices echoed.

Seeing that he was losing out, the Iranian retrieved his sundae and had a go.

"Oh!" His eyes glowed. "God is great," he proclaimed in his native Farsi.

Crayle stepped to where they all could see him as they devoured their treats. "I hereby predict that we shall exit this meeting with a groundbreaking resolution. One that I've taken the liberty to draft."

He passed out the documents.

Just eating noises.

"Oh. Yes. And you are all on video."

• • •

When the word got out that afternoon, the world was shocked. All leaders of religion in the Middle East had agreed on a melding. An aggregation and synthesis of Judaism, Christianity, and Islam. These would become One Religion for the One God.

Crayle also mentioned in his follow-up TV speech that World Peace would become the overarching goal.

Strategist Magus Crayle would lead the development of a formal plan, as well as monitor its progress.

"Religion shall be provided to the masses as guidance only. Those who follow the teaching shall be assessed by the One God alone, since human beings are far subordinated to Him, and unworthy of casting judgment."

• • •

Following a commercial break, Crayle again took the podium for the TV broadcast. The clerics joined him on the set.

"If an individual lived a good life, according to the One God, he or she shall reside in a heavenly paradise for eternity. Their behavior would get them there, not their religion or lack thereof."

"You mean an atheist could finish in Paradise?" asked the Iraqi.

"God is the final arbiter, but He would not reject someone based on ritual behavior, or lack of it. Solely on the goodness of the individual."

"That is blasphemy," the Iranian shouted.

"Blasphemy, like heresy, are words no longer with meaning. Only those who purposefully victimize others should be punished."

The religious leaders waxed quiescent.

"So it is said, so it shall be … and all the clerics," Crayle pointed behind him, "agree."

They remembered the video he'd referenced of them shoveling down bacon.

All nodded.

And all smiled.

CHAPTER 54

The ever available Jack Sommers drove Crayle and Phoebe from the Le Doge, where'd they'd checked out of their room the day following the B Summit, back to the airport.

They knew from before that they had just under an hour to relax. And breathe.

She turned to him. With a smile.

"So, Mr. Crayle. What in heaven's name brought you to Casablanca?"

"My health. I came to Casablanca for the waters."

"The waters? We're in the desert."

She'd teed it up to perfection.

"I was misinformed."

They laughed a full stress expunging laugh.

"Hey, quiet back there. I need my sleep."

"You work for me now, Jack."

"Well then, make all the noise you want."

Phoebe wasn't done.

"You realize you took a chance with those Letters."

"I stick my neck out for no one."

"Except all of us."

She leaned over and pecked him on the cheek.

"Thanks, Mag."

They arrived at the jet.

Luggage on the tarmac next to them, they lingered for a few minutes until the pilot opened the door and rotated the gangway to the ground.

Crayle had felt something in his inside coat pocket the whole time he'd worn it. He reached in a plucked out the contents. He examined his finding. He recognized it immediately. It was a World War II pack of Camel cigarettes his father had shown him long ago.

"So. My mother was in on this, too."

He extracted one and placed it in his mouth. Then, glanced around.

Turning back to Phoebe, he saw her hand rise. She flicked a WWII serviceman's lighter.

He shook his head.

"I don't smoke, but it just seems right."

Then, he heard a voice from behind. From the plane. Marli. Standing in the jet's doorway, she pointed over at a hangar. At a sign.

DÉFENSE ABSOLUE DE FUMER, it read.

"Ah, no smoking."

He replaced the offending item, picked up their luggage, and followed Phoebe aboard.

"Good choice," Marli said. "Captain Louis Renault would've locked you up."

"We're done here. Let me introduce you to the person who's been posing as the French policeman. Phoebe MacKay. Now, and forever after."

• • •

When Flori landed the brand new, not yet in production Dassault Falcon 9X at Washington, D.C.'s Reagan National Airport, she pulled it up and parked next to Marli's 8X.

No sooner had she lowered the gangway, than her two passengers and luggage were on the tarmac with Phoebe sprinting to her husband for a giant hug with Micmac and their child.

And there stood Hekka. With baby Kianna.

Just as Crayle reached them, he heard a familiar sound.

"*Whine!*"

Lenny, Alona, and their little son appeared.

"Let me tell you," Lenny said, "precisely what I was whining about."

"Later, my friend. I know you need some quality time with Alona, so you'll take the 9X with Flori, and we'll ride back with Marli."

"But the president said he needed to see you post haste!"

"The President of the United States of America, and leader of the Free World, is going to have to wait. We're going home."

• • •

The Crayles and MacKays arrived mid-day at Jack Sommers International Airport, or air strip, to find the 9X already there, and Lenny and family departed for their home up the hill in Big Bear Valley.

"Nice of Lenny to wait," Phoebe observed to her husband, with attitude.

"They need to reclaim their lives. Lenny can go back to being a P.I., and Alona can return to her law practice. All while raising little Lenny."

When the Quarry Hospital's ambulance returned, the six of them enjoyed the winding road trip up Highway 18 and around the sizeable Big Bear Lake. The driver, on instructions from Crayle, stopped first at the MacKay cabin. They all trouped inside.

Micmac lifted an acoustic-electric guitar from the stand next to a wall, and settled into a seat on the one armless chair.

Phoebe took notice.

"Oh, we bought a new toy in my absence. Obviously, the lack of motherly oversight."

"It's the most expensive model, too. A Taylor PS12 V-Class Grand Concert Acoustic-Electric. And friendly to the environment." He paused for effect. "Variegated sinker redwood from reclaimed hundred-year-old, Northern California river bottom trees. Matched with figured Tasmanian blackwood—acacia wood similar to Hawaiian koa ..."

"No need to keep all that money around for my needs."

"I was going to put it on Jack's limit free Black Card, but Annie—I mean, Empress Ling—was so grateful, she presented it as a souvenir. Of my trip."

"To keep the new Les Paul she gave you company?"

"Good things come in pairs."

"So, you and Annie?" Phoebe affected a *choose your next words carefully, they might be your last* stare.

"I meant you and I."

Micmac glanced to Crayle, hoping for acknowledgment of a nice save.

Crayle's return look was more of a *I don't know this guy*.

Not good.

Hekka to the rescue with a diversion. "In spite of every bit of energy I use to fight off what we do and what it does to us, I also realize that, given our successes and the degree to which we succeeded, we're in it until the End of Days, as the White Man puts it."

"That would be me," Crayle confessed.

Hekka continued with her rescue mission. "Let's hear it. Play something that's relevant right now."

Micmac began on his new guitar. The opening strains of the Eagles' Hotel California.

It was nice. But everyone wondered, why this song. Until he arrived at the line, *You can check out any time you like, but you can never leave.*

They all knew. It defined their circumstance.

• • •

Back at his cabin with his wife and child for one more final time, Mag Crayle sat in his special chair. It wouldn't win any comfort awards, but it's portability allowed him to trek it in one hand and his fishing gear out to the cabin's dock for some productive, pre-dusk fishing.

The sun pushed West with enough space above the mountains to provide thirty minutes of almost dusk light.

He glanced back toward the cabin. A lot of history there in the past three years. A lot of love had gone on inside.

On cue, Hekka stepped out via the sliding door carrying a tray. Onto the Bar-B-Que plopped the beef patties, the aroma soon wafting his way. He smiled. She could even control the breeze.

Fish or not, there'd be her famous Serrano burgers for dinner.

He wondered. About their first day.

"*Taqt, Taamit, nuht, muat. Taqt, nuht, pat.*"

Words that had been spoken by Hekka's father at the family ranch after she rescued her future husband and soul mate at the Tack Store. They were words of the Serrano Indian language known as Takic.

"Man, sun, woman, moon. Man, woman, water."

The old man had then gone to bed. She'd shown Crayle the waterfall her father had built for her Finnish mother, Helmi. All under a Wolf Moon. A sliver of a moon casting just enough light for a wolf to hunt, but not enough for its prey to be aware.

She had explained this beneath a panorama of a thousand stars.

He later related it to the spy notion of compartmentalization. A project would be defined and designed as separately executable pieces. Those in charge supplied each team with just enough information to complete its mission, but, if captured or spied upon, not enough intel to expose the total mission or its purpose.

He wondered once again.

How could a man love a woman so much?

EPILOGUE

Middle East

A bright light had shown on high over the West coast of Saudi Arabia. Too bright to stare at, but having an incredible magnetism. Witnesses could not look away.

It struck terror into the hearts of the Devil worshipping imams, but wonder and goodness into the hearts of True Believers.

What would a Devil do for maximum pleasure?

Create a religion or co-opt its leaders to present false hope to the faithful while leading them to commit forbidden atrocities, to expose themselves as cowards, and condemn themselves to Eternal Hell, where he, the Devil, would have his way with them. For Eternity.

The True Believers looked at each other without words. The sign from above was clear. The One God was signaling them. The requisite outcome, World Peace, would happen.

They would see to it. They would lead the way.

They would stand in brotherhood, and sisterhood, with all people of the world.

The Russians

Crayle's Blackstone Strategy had been put to use by the czarina. It was simple in concept. Get those standing in your way co-located, then blow them up. It'd gone better than expected for her. The residual Communists of Vladimir's day were in attendance at his mausoleum along with the Illuminé types, the oligarchs, who'd manipulated the others to their own, greed-driven ends. Like Moscow now, they were all gone.

The Indians

Crayle's new client, Rustom Modi of Mumbai, and his beautiful Portuguese heritage wife were finished for the night. She'd moved to her side of the bed, and soon fell fast asleep. He reckoned she still had a smile on her face.

He was too restless to sleep. The czarina had done the deal. With the bomb he'd provided, she eliminated the old Communist faithful and all opposition in Russia. With the same stroke, she wiped out those Russians with tight ties to Iran. Rustom no longer worried about them. Just the Arab-Iranian leadership, the Republican Guard, the Quds force, and, of course, the intelligence entity. With two nuclear devices in his basement, he possessed two major puzzle pieces. Delivery of the first of his original three had tested his transport methodology. It remained for him to develop a reigning structure, to bring in the Iranian and Indian Parsis on his scheme, and to develop a new constitution that would redefine current Iran into the future. A new Persia. Just as Magus Crayle had said.

Rustom Modi had what he wanted. He'd curried favor with the Russians via a gift nuclear bomb to the czarina. Her country's decades long ties to Iranian leaders were what he would need for his Parsi version of a Blackstone Strategy coup. And now he had not just the direct number of master strategist, Magus Crayle, but the number of America's new CIA Director.

The Chinese

Empress Ling's birthday party in Hong Kong went off with a bang. The gentleman flown in from the Guinness Book of World Records rated the individual and then confluent fireworks displays from Victoria Harbour and from Victoria Peak as the biggest and brightest ever. Exhausted and seated back on her throne, she eschewed contemplating the future.

A consort stepped over and softly asked, "What would you like to drink?"

Ling told her.

"That isn't Chinese."

"That's what I want. Dry vodka martini with a twist. Shaken … not stirred."

It arrived forthwith.

She took a sip. Closed her eyes. And leaned back.

She thought of him.

The Vatican

The Pope arrived home following the B Summit in Casablanca. He took the initial thunderstorms' transition to placid flight as a sign. From war and destruction to peace worldwide seemed a new concept. He vowed to apply all of the Vatican resources and every bit of his own energy to the outcome prescribed in so many writings by his Creator, now referred to universally as the One God. He took a moment to wipe a tear, then offered a prayer. For the atheists. He'd respect their views, but would see that they, too, partook of the peace. He completed his prayer with a sigh and a smile.

The Germans

With no nuclear weapons at its disposal and the Made In China channel completely dried up, interest waned. But now the Aryan Alliance had their mini-nuke in exchange for the Iberian boring behemoth, plus on-site technical support. They had to destroy the German government. The American senate-like Bundesrat. The American House of Representatives-like Bundestag. The Chancellor.

The President. The Blackstone Strategy of Herr Crayle required two nuclear weapons. So, how to get them all together at one time became the operative question. Answer: they needed Crayle.

The French

The marriage of Jean-Marc Lalumière, a.k.a. King Louis XX, to the Queen of Sweden completed at the now recreated Notre Dame Cathedral. Those in influence ensured that pomp and circumstance took a back seat to none before. While some Swedes groused that is should have taken place in Stockholm, most were pleased. It was a much needed 'new beginning' for both countries. A renewal of glamour and ostentation.

The Frenchman

Jean-Marc now lived at Versailles with his summer cabin across the way at Fontainebleau. He'd come a long way. He recalled his father initiating him into the Illuminé, the atheist secret society of enlightenment, at the Rocher church near Dabo. At 6'6" he'd towered over the others who, by nature, had to look up to him. He vowed silently—since walls, floor, and ceilings have ears in a palace—to seek the assistance of his one-time arch enemy, Magus Crayle. He needed help in the riddance of any remaining Illuminé. They'd by now be taking victory laps while keeping the new king's secret. That he was an atheist.

They needed to go.

The Iberians

'A river runs through it' didn't quite capture the manifestation of Iberia's new river/canal. Punching the tunnel through at either end ultimately caused a collapse full across the huge peninsula. One could now jet ski from Lisbon all the way to Malaga and back once the effects of major rivers effected, like the Guadalquivir, had leveled themselves out.

In Portugal, with the inversion of the two mini-nukes by Micmac and Crayle, and their detonation, the dreams of Martim Braganza dwindled to nothing. In Spain, the potential of Juan Carlos to become Juan Carlos II, King of Spain, ended with his death. Another nail in the coffin for Illuminé's global domination ambitions. There weren't many nails left. Only one continent remained for a Crayle team destruction of the secret society. Africa.

There was good news, though. The Race to Morocco was such a hit, that a large contingent organized to make it an annual event. The leaders had a plan. They'd just prevail on the American president to have the new CIA chief, Crayle, fire the starting gun. Just not at anyone.

The Americans

President Kimbel Stones was elated. His master chess move at Casablanca paid off. Mag Crayle, his new DCI, pulled it off. The leaders of the three One God religious orders were on board. Already, they attempted to outdo one another in public pronouncements. Each promised a more complete and better peace than the others. Stones considered authorizing a black op to pull them all down. Hadn't they been the problem in the first place? Let's see. Where did he put his hyper-encrypted Smartphone? Ah. There. He touched in Crayle's code.

The Crayles

Back home at their cabin in California's Big Bear Valley, they sat out once again on the back deck facing the lake. The wafting fragrance of Hekka's Serrano burgers never grew old. Magus, Hekka, her mother Helmi, his mother Caitrin, Micmac, Phoebe, Lenny, and Alona plus the three now ambulatory babies comprised the get together.

Next week, Crayle would travel to Langley, hold a high-level meeting with his direct reports, and begin the transformation of the CIA back to its totally-in-the-shadows roots. All while handling the latest passel of world crises.

He'd deliver daily briefings to the president himself. No chance for misinterpretation, and an excuse to see his old friend, Kimbel.

His mind wandered.

How he survived … mentally? What manner of human being could start with the blank mind of an amnesiac, and from month to month receive partial memory restorations? No one could blame him if he climbed into a giant snifter of whisky, and sipped it while treading Scotch. Becoming ever more numb until, at last, he slipped beneath the surface.

To peace.

Everlasting peace.

The Crayles – Goldeneye

Hekka made good on her promise. She whisked the three of them to the former Jamaican residence of spy-novel author, Ian Fleming. When they arrived and settled themselves in, she asked her husband to take a seat, holding the baby, of course.

"I can see you have something to say, my dear Serrano mate. But first, why did you pick five days for us here? Why not three … or seven?"

"Five is a special number. It is the number of children I plan to have by you."

"Hmmm. One down, four to go. We should get started on the rest."

"Always the romantic."

He set the baby in a playpen.

"Let's get started."

Me

This story, like life itself, persists in propelling itself forward. It insinuates itself in my mind such that I am transformed into a mere journalist capturing fictitious political intrigues, relationships, and action.

Series End Plus One

ABOUT THE AUTHOR

Committed to international affairs, political intrigue, and espionage, novelist Dennis Bowen has researched his stories in more than 75 countries. He engenders realism and spice in his thrillers due to his wartime service, and his defense and intelligence community background, which led one reader to remark, "Bowen knows his stuff." *The Gospel Labyrinth* follows *The Water Diamonds*, *The Blackstone Perfection*, *The Crystal Seduction*, *The Redrock Quarantine*, *The Final Masquerade*, *The Virtue Transition*, and *The Jasmine Negative* as the most recent addition to his International Thriller Series. When not traveling the globe to research his next thriller, he resides on the Southern California coast.

Facebook: http://www.facebook.com/DennisBowenThrillers/
Twitter: http://www.twitter.com/DBowenThrillers/
Website: http://www.dennisbowen.com/

AUTHOR'S NOTE

I hope you enjoyed ***The Gospel Labyrinth***. As noted on the cover, this is Book 8 of the ***International Thriller Series***. It stands in addition to the original seven-book series. This note explains, in brief, the process I followed from beginning to end. I decided to include it because there are interesting insights for both readers and aspiring authors.

• • •

How did the original sequential series of seven novels come to be? Prior to my initial writing effort, I would go for bicycle rides around a lake. It was a self-imposed prescription for exercise, fresh air, and a mental time out. Ideas for a story would just pop into my head without any solicitation whatsoever. I'd return home and write them in a notebook. By 2011, I decided to write a novel. The plot would demonstrate how the geopolitical landscape could be severely modified by evil-intentioned malefactors using miniature nuclear devices. I decided to write all the stories in long hand to keep myself physically connected, versus the technological mental distancing inherent with using a computer. After substantial scribblings, annotations, and cross-outs, the words did find their way into the digital orchestration.

Notes on the characters, locations, and scenes grew and grew. I attended a few writers' conferences, read several books, and decided to put pen to paper. So I did. My original estimate, however, would produce a novel of about 750 pages. Too big. I divided the story into three successive novels to make it more manageable, and to provide the initial product to readers much faster.

After three months of putting pen to paper, I realized through epiphany that I'd really gotten to know the story, the settings, and the characters. In fact, I knew the latter so well, I could just keep a mental eye on them, and they could write the scenes. The good news was they couldn't charge me for their efforts. And better yet, I could take all the credit.

As I wrote the three novels, ideas kept coming. By the time I finished them, I had enough notes for two more. Okay, I said. It was meant to be a five novel series. By the time I completed the fifth story, I had notes for two more. The trend led me to pronounce, on more than one occasion, the famous line from the Peanuts cartoon series: Charlie Brown saying, "Good grief!" Or words to that effect. At that point, I considered giving up bicycle riding.

As I noted before, a quite knowledgeable individual whose judgment I trust, deeply familiar with the stories and characters, intimated after reading Book 7, *The Jasmine Negative*, that there just might be an eighth novel required. With ***The Gospel Labyrinth***, I have extended the seven book series.

Once more. "Good grief!"

• • •

Some, including myself, find that in re-reading any of the ***International Thriller Series*** novels, a reader can enjoy them just as much, or even enjoy them more. You can still get everything in normal, silent reading mode, but I suggest you return to a favorite chapter in this story, read it out loud, visualize the characters and observe the difference.

I do perform a great deal of international research since that is the forum in which my stories take place. Although I plan to finally take a little time off, the ideas never stop coming. Fortunately, I did start a second series I called ***The Backstory Files*** in which I took a second-tier individual from the first series and provided how the title character, ***STONES***, transitioned from a National Security Agency operative to Vice President of the United States in an intense, brief period of time. I have many more characters for which I can write thriller back stories.

And with that, best wishes to all those who've supported my efforts, to all those in foreign lands that have provided precious local flavor intel, and finally to every reader on the entire planet. You are why we do this. Seriously. Thank you.

—Dennis Bowen

www.ingramcontent.com/pod-product-compliance
Lightning Source LLC
Chambersburg PA
CBHW020610310726
48979CB00008B/1417/J

* 9 7 8 1 7 3 6 0 2 6 2 0 5 *